A VILLA IN SICILY:

CANNOLI AND A CASUALTY

(A Cats and Dogs Cozy Mystery—Book Six)

FIONA GRACE

Fiona Grace

Debut author Fiona Grace is author of the LACEY DOYLE COZY MYSTERY series, comprising nine books; of the TUSCAN VINEYARD COZY MYSTERY series, comprising seven books; of the DUBIOUS WITCH COZY MYSTERY series, comprising three; of the BEACHFRONT BAKERY COZY MYSTERY series, comprising six books; and of the CATS AND DOGS COZY MYSTERY series, comprising six books.

Fiona would love to hear from you, so please visit www.fionagraceauthor.com to receive free ebooks, hear the latest news, and stay in touch.

A VILLA IN SICILY: OLIVE OIL AND MURDER (Book #1)
A VILLA IN SICILY: FIGS AND A CADAVER (Book #2)
A VILLA IN SICILY: VINO AND DEATH (Book #3)
A VILLA IN SICILY: CAPERS AND CALAMITY (Book #4)
A VILLA IN SICILY: ORANGE GROVES AND VENGEANCE (Book #5)
A VILLA IN SICILY: CANNOLI AND A CASUALTY (Book #6)

CHAPTER ONE

Audrey Smart stood in front of the wall illuminator, reading the X-rays of her latest patient. The results were grim; the answer would not be one that the patient's family would be happy with.

She motioned to Concetta, her assistant. Concetta blinked. "Is that what I think it is?"

Sure enough, the outline was visible in the patient's stomach, right below its ribcage.

"Yep. What it *always* is."

Audrey pulled the X-ray from the board and went to the exam room, where Linda Mancini, another American transplant who'd moved to Mussomeli, Sicily, to take advantage of the one-dollar homes, was worriedly pacing the floor.

"Yes?" she asked when Audrey stepped in and closed the door.

"It's a good thing you brought him in," Audrey explained, clipping the X-ray to the light board and showing the frightened woman the telltale blockage. "Most animals with this condition barely last the day. It's definitely GI stasis. Very common with rabbits."

"Will he be okay?"

"Too early to tell. Unfortunately, rabbit digestive systems are very fragile. It's important to constantly monitor what's going in and out. Things stop up with them, and even if they miss one meal or stop pooping for a morning, you should be worried. We'll need you to start him on Critical Care right away, and I'll provide an antibiotic. You know how to syringe-feed?"

Linda shook her head. "I've only had Grumpy since I moved here three months ago. I found him in my house, living under one of the floorboards."

Poor Grumpy. He'd not had an easy time, it seemed. The one-year-old house rabbit had been abandoned, and now he was facing a health challenge. Linda had woken up this morning to see that Grumpy was lethargic, and hadn't eaten a thing or pooped in hours. That was an instant sign—bunnies were poop machines.

"Okay, well. You simply mix it together with water to make a runny paste, and feed it to him every couple of hours. That should get things moving again. What has he been eating?"

"Carrots, greens, pellets . . ."

"Hay?"

"He doesn't like hay."

"Hay should be a big part of his diet. Bunnies' teeth keep growing, so hay helps wear them down. We filed them some so that he'd stop making that clicking noise you were concerned about, which might mean he's in pain, but the hay will do it naturally. Only give carrots sparingly, as they're high in sugar. What kind of greens?"

"Oh, whatever I pick up at the store. Lettuce. Broccoli . . ."

"Lettuce is good; try Romaine. Steer clear of broccoli. Most bunnies love it but it does give them gas."

"Oh, okay. Perfect, thanks," she said, as Concetta came in with the animal in his pet carrier.

"And keep in mind that bunnies are prey animals. They are used to hiding their afflictions from others, even their owners, so as not to appear too weak and defenseless."

"Ohhh, don't you worry, my little Grumpy bun!" Linda said in baby voice, lifting the carrier and touching her nose to the animal's. "You're going to be just fine! I am going to baby you like no tomorrow!"

The veterinarians ushered her out to the front lobby, where they said goodbye. When Audrey closed the door, she flipped the sign to *CHIUSO*, closed, and yawned, stretching her arms up over her head. Then she pulled off her white coat and draped it over the chair in the reception area. "Long day."

"Tell me about it," Audrey's model-pretty young protégé said, pulling off her apron. "Do you want me to finish up with the billing? I still have a few I haven't sent out yet, and a couple of checks that need to go to the bank."

Audrey shook her head. "Tomorrow is Saturday. They're open Saturdays, right? Do it then."

She winced as she scanned the place. After a long, busy day, it looked like it usually did . . . dingy. And it smelled worse. The back room had to be cleaned, but the animals had been fed and cuddled and walked, and if she didn't leave now, she'd always find more things to do.

And her little home at *Piazza Tre* needed attention, too. She'd gotten most of the rooms on the first floor renovated, but that still left the bedrooms, and she was planning to tile the upstairs bathroom tonight. "I have things to do at home."

Concetta raised an eyebrow. "Mason helping you?"

Audrey's stomach tightened at the thought of her contractor neighbor, another American transplant. "No. I can actually do things myself, without him!"

"Yes, but he's so *sexy*." She made the dreamy face most women made when they saw her handsome Southern handyman neighbor. "If it were me, I'd want his help as much as possible. As often as possible. And you make a cute couple."

She winced. Mason was cute, and he knew it, but their last "date," if it could be called that, had been really, well . . . weird. She'd had too much on her mind, and he'd seemed more awkward, too. They'd been dancing back and forth for months about getting together, but never seemed to make it work. The last date, she'd hoped it would move things forward. That he'd at least attempt to kiss her.

Instead, he'd gone on and on about her new mafia friends, the Piccolo family. Audrey had originally had no intention of getting involved with the mob, but after helping to solve a case at their estate outside the Mussomeli city limits, she'd become the darling of the entire Piccolo family. They'd invited her to a family gathering outside of the city, in a town west of Mussomeli.

Mason had made it clear, in no uncertain terms, that he thought going would be a big mistake. He kept warning her, over and over again, to be careful. He'd even told her outright that she shouldn't go. *Trust me, you don't want to get involved with those clowns,* he'd said.

But what did Mason, a South Carolina boy, know about the Sicilian mob? No, Audrey had the feeling his reluctance had more to do with one clown in particular.

Rafael Piccolo.

Rafael was handsome, thoughtful, and romantic. A real charmer. Audrey sensed some real jealousy there. Mason seemed jealous whenever *any* other male talked to her, and while that flattered her, sometimes it was outright annoying and childish.

So Audrey didn't want to see Mason, even just to have him help her with her sad upstairs bathroom. Not now, the day before she was due to leave for the weekend gathering. One look in those mesmerizing blue eyes, and she'd probably agree to anything he asked for.

"He's so cute, and he knows it. He's also a pain in the butt," she pointed out.

3

"You always say that!" Concetta exclaimed, grabbing her bag.

She shrugged. "Because it's true."

"Which reminds me . . ." Concetta said, her eyes widening. "What about that Piccolo guy? The one from the orange groves. Are you going to accept the invitation?"

Audrey shrugged. She'd been staring at the invitation every day for three weeks. She'd gone back and forth on it. Despite his jealousy, Mason was probably right—it could be dangerous. She could easily make the excuse that she was too busy with work and her house. But then again, she'd come out here to experience Sicilian culture. When would she ever have such an opportunity again?

"I don't know. I shouldn't leave. I have animals who need me. Animals like Grumpy . . ."

"But you have me. And I can take care of anything."

That was true. Concetta was more than capable. "What do you think I should do? I should give him an answer tonight because the event is this weekend."

"Where is it again?"

"In Corleone. Do you know where that is?"

"It's about an hour west of here. Well, you know, if you wanted to go, I would of course mind the vet center. Luca could help me. I think we would have no trouble. But . . ." She shook her head. "I don't think I'd do it. Being that far away from home with a bunch of strangers?"

Audrey smiled. She'd come here to this town in the middle of Sicily, all alone, five months ago. It had been a last-minute, change-of-pace thing, something to shake her life up a little. And shake things up, it had. She'd experienced so much of a new culture, met all kinds of interesting people. It'd definitely been worth it. "I have experience in that, actually. And I don't know. A new adventure might be fun."

"I'm sure it would be," she said doubtfully. "But this isn't just any kind of adventure. My parents tell me all kinds of stories about the mafia, from when I was born. They are not very nice people."

"Oh, but I know Rafael. And he's not a bad person. And though his family might be a little shady, I don't know if he personally is involved."

"How well do you know him? He just moved to Mussomeli last month."

Audrey had accidentally met him when she wandered into his place on the edge of town. Since then, she'd gone over to his estate, among the orange groves, a few times for lunch. He'd been charming, though a

4

bit secretive. And there were always men in suits and sunglasses coming and going in black sedans. Every time she left his house, she always had the feeling he was in the middle of something not-quite-legal.

She nodded. "You're right. I should turn it down. He is a nice man. He'll understand."

Concetta nodded and headed for the door. "Probably for the best. Have a great night!"

Audrey followed soon afterward. Her pet fox, Nick, waited for her on the stoop, licking his paws. "My bodyguard," she said, stooping and giving him a rub between the ears.

Then she looked up and down the street and shivered. Maybe it was the rash of murders around the area since she arrived, or maybe it was the rumor that the mafia had come back to Mussomeli, but she couldn't help feeling like something terrible was about to happen.

And once again, she'd probably be caught in the middle of it.

"I'm overreacting," she said aloud, taking the first step toward home.

CHAPTER TWO

Audrey loved the quaint little town nestled in the hills of Sicily, with its crooked cobblestone streets, its small markets, homes with lines full of laundry hung from the second-floor windows, and friendly people. Most of all, the friendly people. She waved hello to her teenage friend Luca, who was pulling in a barrel of rakes in from outside the hardware store, and some other smiling faces as she passed.

"*Buona sera!*" she said to them all. She'd come to Sicily not knowing a word of Italian, much less Sicilian. But over the months, with friendly people to guide her, she'd learned enough to get by.

When she passed her favorite café, La Mela Verde, it was busy as usual, the line waiting for a table stretching out the open front door. Through it, she spotted G behind the host's podium by the doors.

"*Ciao, bella!*" he shouted to her, always the charmer. "Coming in for some of your favorite *ciambotta*?"

Her mouth watered at the thought. But with that crowd to contend with? She'd never get home at a decent hour. He usually had a few spots open for single diners at the bar, and his place was full of all the charm of Sicily—with bottles of wine and grapevines for décor—but right now, all she could think about was getting back to her little renovation project.

"Not tonight!" she called back. "Maybe later this week!"

"Promise? *Principessa*, I don't know if I can go much longer without seeing your smiling face at my counter!"

"I promise! But I am sure you'll survive," she said with a laugh, continuing on. G had his share of female admirers, that was for sure.

It was a good thing that his café was too crowded to stop at. Earlier this month, she'd made a pledge to be a little more independent, not relying on the men in her life for help with her house or chores. She'd been bouncing back and forth between G and Mason since she got here, and it had been enough to make her dizzy. Adding Rafael to the mix hadn't helped. Though she was in her thirties, and the biological clock was ticking, she'd made peace with the idea of just focusing on herself for now—the vet business, the house. Men need not apply.

She stopped at il Mercado de Pepe and got a pint of her favorite *Macco di fave*, a traditional bean soup, a loaf of crusty semolina, and of course, an apple for Nick. Saying good night to the DeMauro family, who ran the shop, she quickly headed off toward her stately row-home in mid-town Mussomeli, located at *Piazza Tre.*

The second she rounded the corner and her home came into view, so did the cameras. They clogged the narrow street like bees swarming around a hive. Blinded by a bright floodlight, Audrey stumbled a bit on the uneven cobblestones as she forged her way to her door, holding tight to her precious dinner.

For a second, she almost expected Spielberg to pop out, because that's what it looked like at *Piazza Due*, directly across the street from Audrey's house—a major movie production. Her neighbor, Nessa, was filming a home remodeling show for HGTV. That would've been exciting, if not for the cameras pointed at Audrey's house at all hours of the day. Sometimes, *in* her house—she'd actually caught a few of the crew peeking in her windows with their cameras.

Not to mention that Nessa had a bit of a strong personality. The California bombshell made no secret of the fact that she didn't like Audrey very much. In fact, their first meeting, Nessa had accused Audrey of murder—a charge that had very nearly sent Audrey to prison for the rest of her life.

"Cut! Cut!" Nessa's voice screeched from somewhere. Audrey wasn't sure where, because of the temporary blindness. All she knew was that, surprise, surprise, Nessa didn't sound happy.

Audrey had a good feeling that it was probably something she had done. "Sorry," she mumbled preemptively, cringing as she reached her front stoop and fumbled for her keys. "If you just let me get inside, I'll—"

Somewhere, closer, she heard Nessa snarl, "So? What do you have to say for yourself?"

Audrey blinked away the starbursts in her vision to find the blonde, heavily made-up for filming, staring at her, hands on her hips, toe tapping. She was wearing an apron and holding a hand spade, as if she intended to commit murder with it.

"Hi, Nessa!" Audrey said brightly. "How's Snowball?"

Nessa seemed surprised by the sweetness in her tone. "She's fine. Just fine."

Audrey still wasn't fully convinced that Nessa hadn't adopted the pure white kitten just to add another point of interest to her reality

7

show, since the show was Nessa's life. She barely spoke of anything else. "That's good to hear."

"Don't change the subject," she groused, pointing at the camera crew. "You walked right into our frame!"

"I'm sorry. I didn't know you were filming."

"Of course I was. Aren't I always? All these cameras hanging around didn't give it away? And it was finally perfect until you and your big nose walked into it."

Audrey touched her nose. No, it was a tiny little upturned ski-slope like Nessa's, but she didn't think it was *big*. "Sorry, but I *do* need to get to my house from time to time."

"You have a back door, don't you? And there's an alley over there, right? We've done this take fifteen times," Nessa muttered, pointing to one of the flower beds that was half-planted with roses.

"Fifteen? I thought these reality television shows were supposed to be unscripted?"

Nessa rolled her eyes as if to say, *amateurs*. "Daylight's gone now. Oh well." She clapped her hands. "Come on, guys! Make-up? Do I look okay? Get me some powder. I feel shiny. Let's get this next take lined up!"

Escaping, Audrey went quickly to her stoop with her key at the ready. She unlocked the door and went inside, nearly clipping off Nick's tail as he trailed in behind her. As she closed the door, she heard Nessa speaking in an unusually chipper voice to the camera. "Working in the garden is one of my favorite ways to relax! I absolutely love planting my roses once the sun goes down and it's not so hot!"

Audrey shook her head, happy to close out the sounds of the filming outside. She went to the kitchen table and cut the apple for Nick, leaving it in his bowl. In the dishrack, she found a spoon and pulled off the top of her bean soup, inhaling the savory scent of it.

Sitting down at the kitchen bistro table, taking a scoop of it, she pulled out her phone to text Rafael. She'd just written half the message: *I'm sorry, but I can't* when someone rapped on the door.

"It's open," she called, hoping it wasn't Nessa again.

When the door pushed open, though, a gigantic beast filled the doorway, then rushed forward into her arms, nearly knocking her from the table. Somewhere, Nick hissed and scurried off. Her soup went flying to the ground as she was covered in warm, wet dog kisses.

"Polpetto!" she whined. Ordinarily, she'd have loved dog kisses—she was a vet, after all. But her beautiful soup. She stared at it, splattered on the ground and her lap, not mourning so much that she'd have to clean it up but that she'd desperately wanted it in her belly.

On cue, her stomach growled.

She grabbed the giant mastiff by the collar and stared at the open door. "Uh, Mason?" she called.

A second later, her *GQ*-cover-gorgeous friend appeared. "Hey, Boston," he said, pointing out the door. "Just chatting with Nessa. She ain't so happy with Polpetto. Messed up her shot."

"She's not happy with anyone," Audrey pointed out, blotting at the hot liquid seeping into her pants.

"She seems to like me okay." He winked.

Audrey's heartstrings gave a sad twang. Nessa had as much charm as a shark, but she was just beautiful enough that it didn't matter. Men seemed to flock to her anyway. She hated the thought of Mason, her dear friend, being taken in by that. "Oh. Close the door before the insects get in."

"Sure, I—" He suddenly noticed her and the mess as he bumped the door shut. "Whoa, girl. You don't look right. What happened to you?"

"Ya think? An uncontrolled Polpetto happened to me."

His mouth made an O. He took the giant dog by the collar and wagged a finger at him. "What I tell you, boy? You don't do things like that."

Polpetto's excited tail-wagging ceased and he hung his head.

"Aw," Audrey said. She never could stand the sight of a scolded pup. She took his face in her hands and started to rub his big jowls. "Don't worry, little Polpie. It's okay. You're forgiven."

The excited wagging resumed, and when she let him go, he started to lap up the soup from the floor with his massive tongue.

"Besides," she added, "your owner should've been watching over you a little better."

Mason winced. "Sure, make me the bad guy," he said, watching him eat. "That gonna hurt him?"

She shook her head. "At least someone should enjoy it. He's probably going to do a better job than my mop."

"Sorry about that. Which reminds me," he said, pulling a little tray out from behind his back. "Had this left over from my dinner tonight."

Audrey's mouth started to water as the smell of bacon hit her. The only thing she liked more than ciambotta and bean soup was Mason Legare's famous down-home southern cooking. She sniffed some more. "Is that what I think it is?"

"Kentucky Hot Brown."

"Yum!" She clapped her hands and practically pounced on it, determined to have her way with it before Polpetto did. "Thank you. I'll almost forgive you for ruining my outfit."

He looked down at it and rubbed the back of his neck. "Yeah. About that. Sorry."

She smiled at the gentlemanly way he averted his eyes when she shrugged off her shirt. There was nothing inappropriate about it—she was wearing a T-shirt underneath. But he always did things like that, surprising, thoughtful things that most men wouldn't think to do.

If only I was more like my older sister, Sabrina, when it came to men, she thought. *He'd be eating out of the palm of my hand by now.*

It seemed like their relationship was full of stops and starts, so even though he was her closest friend in Sicily, there was still so much awkwardness between them. She hated that they couldn't seem to ever be in the same place when it came to dating. There was always something getting in the way. "It's all right. Would you like some wine?"

He nodded. "Now you're speaking my language."

She hopped over Polpetto's sleeping body—he'd devoured the food and conked out on the rug—and grabbed the wine from the shelf, pouring each of them a glass.

But if I had been like my sister, she thought as she placed the wine in front of Mason, *I'd be content with Boston, and married with two kids by now. I'd never have even thought about moving to Sicily.*

And that would've been a shame. Though she'd had her share of travesties, it had been, for the most part, a good experience.

"What are you thinking?" he said before taking a sip.

She smiled. "Oh. Just about all the amazing things that have happened in the past few months. Like opening the vet office, getting all those pets adopted, learning Sicilian culture, making this house into a home . . ."

He nodded. "Meeting me . . ."

"Of course," she said with a laugh, digging into her delicious Hot Brown. Mouth full, she said, "Can't forget that."

There was a long silence as she devoured her food. Meanwhile, Mason just watched her, which was a little uncomfortable. She was about to ask him how his day was when he added, "And your run-in with the mafia. That was a big, red-letter moment."

Audrey's smile fell and she winced. She knew he would find a way to swing the conversation around to that. She just *knew* it. "Yes . . ."

"So," he said innocently, and she knew exactly what the next words out of his mouth were going to be. "You make any decisions on that invitation you got? Where was that family gathering again? Corsica?"

"Corleone," she muttered, taking a sip from her wine. She looked at her food. The conversation wasn't enough to make her lose her appetite—she could *never* lose her appetite where Kentucky Hot Browns were concerned—but close. "I know you think it's dangerous, but I came here for new—"

"Yeah, you've done some pretty crazy things in your time here, girl, but if you go to that, you got to be plumb stupid," he said with a nod. "You better make sure you say your goodbyes before you go, 'cause there's a good chance you ain't coming back."

"Oh, come on. Rafael is not that bad!" she said. Again, Audrey couldn't tell what was jealousy, and what was mere concern over her well-being. "His family didn't invite me just so they could off me. What would be the purpose in that? They invited me because they *like* me. They appreciate me and want to thank me. As bad as the mafia is, they actually don't go around killing people they like."

"So you are going." His face fell.

She opened her mouth to tell him that she'd made the decision not to go.

But then he said, "I'm tellin' you, it's a mistake."

She gnashed her teeth. Just who did he think he was, telling her what she could and couldn't do? He couldn't even bring himself to kiss her. Just one, stupid kiss. And yet he wanted to dictate her life? They weren't even *dating*.

"But maybe it's not."

"Maybe it is."

She stared him down. *Just one little kiss. Give me one little kiss, and maybe I'll all but forget that trip.* But he just pushed away from the desk, his body rigid, so rigid, she could see the tight, corded muscles flexing in his biceps.

Just then, someone else rapped on the door, and Polpetto jumped to attention, barking up a storm.

"Shh, Polpy," she said, calming him as she nudged past him to the foyer.

She opened the door to find Rafael himself standing there with a basket of oranges.

"Oh! Rafael! How nice to see you!" she gushed, just to drive it home that Mason had no say in what she did or didn't do. "Come in."

She took the oranges from him and beamed at them. Truthfully, she hated oranges, but she hadn't been able to tell Rafael that after the last three buckets he delivered. Though she really couldn't imagine a man like Rafael, who probably wore suits to bed, standing outside in the blazing sun, picking the oranges by hand—he likely hired people for that—it had been a nice thought. She'd simply thanked him and quietly distributed the fruit among her neighbors.

He stepped inside, all smiles, until he saw Polpetto, who growled at him, and Mason, who wasn't much better. His posture was rigid as he stood up.

"Oh," Rafael said, still pleasantly, but with a slight edge. "I didn't know you had company."

"We were just leaving," Mason grumbled, glaring at Audrey. The temperature in the room seemed to skyrocket.

Audrey sighed. "Mason, don't be silly. You don't have to go anywhere. We're all neighbors, here."

"No, no, I've got things to do anyway," he said, clearly determined to leave no matter what she said. "I'll see you later."

And though he went through the door without another word, she was sure he had *plenty* he wanted to say to her.

But no kiss. And without the kiss, she decided, she was free to make her own decisions about what she did or didn't do when it came to the Piccolos' invitation.

12

CHAPTER THREE

Audrey wasn't an expert on the mafia, but if she had to pick out a mobster from a line-up, Rafael, with his dark suit, tousled black hair, and sharp features, would probably be her first choice. Even now, though they were friends, his presence made her tongue-tied and anxious. Well, she was *usually* tongue-tied and anxious around men, but Rafael Piccolo took that to a whole new level. It was nothing he did, so much as just knowing that he was from a powerful mafia family.

She tucked a lock of hair behind her ear and smiled at him. "So, to what do I owe the pleasure?"

"I can't drop by simply to deliver my bounty?" he asked with a wink, pointing at the oranges.

She knew there was more to it than that. Every time he'd come into town, he'd asked her questions about the town, quizzing her. She had a feeling that he had other motives. She just wasn't sure what they were. "Oh, you can. But the walk from your grove up to town is five hundred steps, straight up. It's not exactly easy. There has to be more to it than that."

He smiled. "You are right. Do you not remember what I asked you before?"

She suddenly realized what it was. Last time he'd brought her oranges, he'd said, *I will be waiting with bated breath for your answer.*

Her stomach sank. Why had she brought it up?

"Yes, I do . . ." she said, her eyes trailing to the floor. What were the chances a meteor would strike and she wouldn't have to answer? She pretended to be distracted by something in the kitchen. "Oh! Uh, where are my manners? I was just having wine and finishing my dinner. Would you like some?"

He nodded and sat down in the chair across from her that had previously been Mason's. She took away Mason's glass and filled a new one for Rafael. As she did, she caught him eyeing her plate.

"That's a Hot Brown," she explained. "Or, part of one. Mason's always delivering his southern food to me because he knows I work late."

"How nice of him."

"Yes, he's a good friend." She sat across from him and noticed he was wearing loafers without socks, a look no American would ever get away with. And yet, it fit him. He seemed so comfortable, even in his suit.

She started to dig into the rest of her food, avoiding his eyes, when he reached out and grabbed her hand. "Audrey."

She had no choice but to look at him. "Hmm?"

"Audrey, you're avoiding the question. Why?"

She bit her tongue. "I'm not, I'm just . . ."

"I will ask you again. My family invited you to their home for their family reunion, at my request. I'm leaving tomorrow morning for Corleone. I wanted to know if you'd like to drive over with me."

She looked into his eyes. He'd requested it. As much as she'd have liked to believe that this was just because she'd helped him out with that little scrape last month, when he looked at her this way, held her hand like this, she thought it had to be something else.

Thus, her confusion. Why couldn't the men in her life just say what they meant, for once? "I know. I've been thinking about it, but . . ."

"If you are afraid that I will take advantage of you, please be assured that you will be perfectly safe. My whole family will be there, most you already know from that dinner. You will like them all, and enjoy it tremendously."

"Your whole family will be there?"

"Yes. Some of them are Americans, like you, too. We all speak English. Do not worry that you won't find friends. You will fit right in. Trust me."

She managed a smile. "It's not that. I'm just so busy. With renovations around here, and . . . of course there's the vet. I am the only one in town, so it's difficult for me to break away."

This was all untrue. Sure, she had those things to worry about, but the renovations could wait a couple of days. And Concetta had told Audrey that if she wanted to go, she should. The young vet student was more than capable of handling the center for a few days. There were no pressing engagements keeping her from saying yes.

But as much as she hated to admit it, Mason was right. And Concetta had confirmed it. She was right to feel uneasy. She should've put her foot down and declined the invitation weeks ago. Now, she was in the hotseat, and with him looking at her that way, it was hard to back out.

He shook his head and made a tutting sound. "Just for one weekend, really?"

"One weekend is a very long time in the veterinary business. I have a bunny with GI stasis, and—"

"Yes, but it's just two days. You come Saturday. Then right back on Sunday evening. Yes?"

She frowned and began to shake her head. "Well, as much as I like it—"

"My grandfather, Don Piccolo, our esteemed patriarch, personally requested your presence, you know, with my father, Carmine, the acting don. They would both be deeply offended if you said no."

"Yes, but if you explained to them—"

"An invitation like that, one from on high, is not something you turn down," he interrupted, shaking his head. "There is no explanation that will satisfy either of those men. They are used to getting whatever they request. You see?"

"But I—"

He gazed at her with such intensity that she could sense a hidden meaning. A horrible scene flashed in front of her eyes—men in dark suits, beating down her door and dragging her into the streets, sneering. "Don Piccolo requested your attendance and you dishonored our family! Death to you and all you love!"

She shivered at the thought.

Her attendance at this family reunion wasn't just requested.

It was mandatory.

That was why he'd been coming around, lightly coaxing her to say yes. Now, it was a demand. She had no choice. "If I need to be there, why didn't you just say so?"

He shrugged. She got the feeling there was a lot of innuendo in his family, a lot of rules that were unspoken but instinctively obeyed if a person knew what was good for him. Maybe that was why she still had no clue if he was romantically interested in her, or just trying to get her to come so they wouldn't have to deal with the messy task of gunning her down in the middle of the street. "So I will pick you up tomorrow? Say eleven?"

She nodded and swallowed, then pushed her plate away. Now, she really was no longer hungry. "Sounds like a plan. I will be ready."

*

As Audrey knelt, hunched down, near the upstairs toilet, trying to fit a cut tile into the space behind it, she groaned. Only fifteen minutes in, and every muscle in her back and legs hurt from the strange contortions she was doing to fit the pieces of tile into the right places.

"I am dying," she muttered to no one in particular, straightening and massaging her lower back. As she did, she noticed Nick perched on the sink console, peering at her curiously. "You don't do tile, do you? You're smaller than me. If you could just fit under there with a little grout on your paws, you could really help me out . . ."

He hissed and scampered off.

"Yep. Thanks for your help, Bub."

She grabbed her bottle of water and took a swig, then sat on the toilet seat, looking around. She was going to paint the room the color of old parchment, and had little rose-speckled curtains for the single window over the clawfoot bathtub. It would look great once it was finished.

When this room was done, she'd be nearly at the home stretch. All she'd have was her bedroom. She'd had such fun picking out the mauve paint for that room, and choosing the right hardwood for the floor. But that shouldn't take more than another month. Then she'd be done.

Sadness unexpectedly crept in.

And then what? What happened afterwards?

As hard as it was, it was also kind of depressing to know that her home would be done. Sure, she could give the outside a coat of paint, work in the garden, but . . . as frustrating as all of it had been and as much as she complained about it, when she didn't have it to deal with . . . she had a feeling she'd miss it.

And sure, things were exciting now, but that was because she had so much pulling on her. So many things that needed to be done. But once the house was done, once Concetta became a licensed vet, what would come next? What was the next chapter in her life?

She wasn't sure.

I'm just feeling nervous because of what's about to happen tomorrow, she thought. Ever since Rafael's visit, she hadn't been able to think of anything but the trip.

Audrey bristled at a vision of walking down the aisle with Rafael, followed by a man with a machine gun pointed at her back. What if this was just the start of things, and it was too late? What if they forced her into marrying into the family? *An invitation like that, one from on high, is not something you turn down.*

She gagged at the thought. Rafael was perfectly nice and handsome, though a bit frightening, but his *family*? They were downright petrifying.

And she was going to spend the whole weekend with them.

So who knew what came next, after the house was done? Maybe she'd never have a chance to find out. Maybe she'd go to this thing tomorrow and never return.

This was definitely the stuff of one of those one-hour true crime series.

"Tonight on *Unsolved Mysteries*," she mumbled to herself, doing her best Robert Stack impersonation. "She went into the idyllic town of Corleone, Sicily, for a simple weekend away from her day-to-day drudgery. But then she disappeared without a trace! What happened to American veterinarian Audrey Smart?"

The thought made her feel ill. Ill enough to fake a sickness and spend the whole weekend in bed, at home.

But was this home? Even though she'd covered it with her colors, her décor, something about it still felt foreign. Not like hers. Even after all this time, all the work she'd done and all the friends she'd made, she had to admit . . . she still felt a little like an outsider.

Maybe it was just that the vet center was practically overrun with animals, and she still had bills to pay on it. Or that the house, as well as it was coming along, had been a lot of work and yet still wasn't perfect. Or that none of the men in her life seemed to be able to say what they meant around her.

Mason should've kissed me.

She shoved the thought away. *If he hasn't done it in five months, he probably never will.*

Besides, maybe taking the weekend and being with the Piccolos would make her feel like part of a family. She'd never had that before.

But did she want this particular family to welcome her in? That was the question. The Piccolos were probably a lot like a roach motel—you can get in, but you can't get out.

Ever.

Shivering more at that thought, she wiped the sweat from her brow and stood up, peering at herself in the cracked mirror. She needed a new one. That thing was not only cracked, but she could barely see her reflection anymore in the surface.

But renovations would have to wait for now. She needed to start packing for tomorrow. Grabbing her phone, she texted Concetta:

Wanted to let you know I decided to accept the invitation and I'm going to Corleone for the weekend. Can you fill in?

Concetta: Of course! But . . . :0

Audrey: I know, I know! It'll be fine. I'm sure. I'll call Linda from the road to see how Grumpy is doing. And if I don't show up on Monday. . .

Concetta: Don't say that! You'll be fine. Have a great time. I'll call if I need anything.

Thank goodness for Concetta. Over the past couple of months, she'd really turned into Audrey's right hand.

Standing there with her phone, she wondered if she should let anyone else know.

Mason, mostly.

Then she decided against it. He'd only try to convince her what a bad idea it was, and make her feel even more nervous.

Plus, he hadn't kissed her . . .

She found herself dragging her feet as she went to her bedroom and pulled her suitcase out from under her bed, then took the weekend bag out from inside it. Opening it, she tapped her finger against her chin, trying to decide what to wear. *What do mafia people wear? What's the weather going to be like? Where is Corleone, anyway?*

Well, she could answer at least a few of those questions. She picked up her phone and typed in Corleone weather. The first thing that showed up was a small paragraph about the city: *Several mafia bosses have come from Corleone. It is also the birthplace of several fictional characters in Mario Puzo's* The Godfather, *including the eponymous Vito Corleone.*

Great. Corleone, Sicily: All mafia, all the time.

But good news: It had a warm and temperate climate with relatively dry weather.

She filled her bag with her necessities, trying to keep the dread at bay.

Stop it, Audrey, be happy! You are going on a great adventure! A family reunion! There'll be food, companionship, dancing, and . . .

Guns. And drugs. And racketeering, whatever that is. Maybe even a couple of murders.

She shook that thought away. After all, in the past few months, she'd found herself in plenty of bad situations, and they'd all worked in her favor, eventually.

She'd just have to find a way to make sure this weekend worked in her favor, too.

CHAPTER FOUR

The following morning was a bright and sunny one. When Audrey pushed open the shutters to the large picture window in her bedroom, she took in deep breaths of cool, dewy air, and stared as the sun spread its rays upon Mussomeli Castle and the orange groves below. The weather reports forecast clear skies and eighty-degree temperatures for the entire weekend.

It's going to be a beautiful day! she thought to cheer herself, as Nick hopped into her arms, demanding to be stroked. *If I can survive it.*

Trying not to think all those thoughts of doom and gloom, especially during such a glorious day, she quickly showered and dressed in capris and a nice sweater, and lugged her weekend bag downstairs. As she was chopping up some snacks to put in Nick's pet carrier, someone knocked on the door.

She checked her phone. Eleven, exactly.

Those mafia people sure were punctual.

Taking a deep breath, she opened the door. Rafael stood there, in his blazer and white dress shirt open at the throat, showing a gold chain with a cross on it. His hair was wet and slicked back from his face, and he had dark sunglasses on.

"*Ciao, Bella,*" he said, a smile spreading on his face. "Are you ready?"

She nodded and handed him the pet carrier, then reached for her other bag. "Yes, if you just take this, I'll get my other things, and then we can be on the—"

"So you are bringing your fox, eh?"

She nodded. "I can't go anywhere without him," she explained, which was not exactly true. He'd been injured, and wound up following her around once she nursed him to health, and though she'd come to depend on the little animal to keep her company, he'd likely be perfectly fine on his own, on the streets, for the next few days. "Is that a problem?"

She was hoping he'd say yes, that his grandfather was allergic, and that she'd have to stay home. But instead he smiled and put the carrier in the back of his Mercedes convertible. "Of course not. The more, the merrier."

As she locked the door, she looked up and down the street. Thankfully, Nessa and her filming pals had cleared out, and the street was empty. When she got to the car door, Rafael swept in, ever the gentleman, and opened it for her, settling her inside. "Thank you."

Rafael took the narrow street to the main piazza, then turned left, heading out of the city. Her cinnamon hair blew into her face, so she quickly pulled it into a ponytail. Soon, they were going up and down among the grassy, rolling hills of the countryside, and Audrey's ears were popping like crazy. Rafael leaned in to say something, but she didn't hear because of her clogged ears and the rushing wind. "What did you say?" she yelled.

"I said I've been making inquiries into your father!" he yelled back.

"Oh?" she said, allowing hope to flutter in her stomach. Her father had been her best friend, growing up in Boston. He'd been her greatest champion, and a contractor, too, who'd taught her everything she knew about fixing up an old house. It was his spirit of adventure, and his appetite for fixing old, broken things, wearing off on Audrey, that had probably led her to Sicily in the first place.

But then Miles Smart had disappeared without a trace, without a single word to Audrey. Audrey was only a young teenager when he walked out of her life forever. Sabrina had been bitter about it, but not Audrey. She'd desperately wanted to talk to him, to find out what had driven him away from her. She'd been trying to find him ever since, with no luck.

But Rafael had given her hope. He'd said he had connections that spanned the globe, that specialized in finding those who didn't want to be found. And if the mafia was able to do things that other people technically couldn't, maybe Rafael and his people could finally succeed where she had failed.

When she saw the look on his face, though, all her hope drained away. He shook his head. "I'm sorry. So far, nothing. I called on a couple of friends that lived in Montagnanera, but neither of them knew a Miles Smart who lived there. One knew an American who lived in town, but it was not the same person. I also looked into some other possible Miles Smarts, but they were not the same person. It's possible he changed his name." Pity clouded his eyes. "I wish I had better news."

21

"It's all right," she said. Truthfully, she didn't know how she'd even react if she ever did meet her father again. Would she feel complete? Would she blubber like a total mess? Or would she be angry? It was probably better this way. "Thank you for trying."

"But I have only just begun. I will keep on digging, checking into other resources I have," he said, patting his leather steering wheel. "So cheer up. I have many more leads I can follow. I am not done."

She shook her head. "I don't know. Maybe you should just stop. If he changed his name . . . Maybe he left because he wants to stay lost."

"From you, charming girl? I doubt it," he said, giving her a brilliant smile. "I am sure he would be proud of you for the woman you have become. A doctor, and a beautiful one at that."

She felt herself heating from head to toe. Was he flirting with her? Sometimes she couldn't tell.

The image of her in a wedding dress, with the barrel of a gun pointed between her shoulder blades, popped into her head. She forced it out.

"Thank you. I'm excited to meet the rest of your family," she said, looking over her shoulder to check on Nick. "Your grandfather will be there?"

"Oh yes, and they'll all be excited to meet you."

Nick seemed a little agitated, pressing his nose up against the door, but he never did like his carrier. She stuck a finger in and petted his head. "They know that I'm coming?"

"Of course! You are going to be our guest of honor."

She gritted her teeth. She hated that kind of attention. "Guest of honor? Why?"

"Well, because word gets around about how you saved my family from any embarrassment regarding the murder that happened at my estate. We are all eternally grateful for your assistance in that matter."

"That was nothing," she said with a wave, though it had been quite the adventure. It had involved gunplay, threats, kidnapping . . . basically all the typical mafia stuff she hoped to avoid for the rest of her life. "How many people will be there?"

"At my grandfather's estate? Not many. Ninety . . . one hundred people?"

Her jaw dropped. "You're kidding. All family?"

He shrugged. "I have a big family. My father is one of thirteen children."

"Oh my god. And surely not all of them know about me?" That whole *guest of honor* thing had to be an exaggeration. She really *hoped* it was an exaggeration.

"They all do! My grandfather can't wait for you to come, and my father especially wants to meet you. Carmine, his name is. He is the true don, the head of the business, now that my grandfather's health has been declining."

The last time Audrey had seen Don Piccolo, he'd barely looked at her from across the table at this big celebratory dinner they had. He probably couldn't have even *seen* her across the table. He was so old, probably about ninety, frail, likely only a shadow of the man he once was.

She could deal with an old man, even if he was mafia. But Carmine, his son? Audrey had to admit, if he was anything like Rafael, she'd probably be shaking in her shoes. She'd been *so* intimidated the first time she met Rafael.

"Well, I can't wait to see them. But I don't think I'm going to be able to remember the names of all your family."

"That's all right. I barely remember them myself." He reached over the console and patted her arm. "You'll be fine."

She had begun to relax a little bit, but the moment he touched her, the butterflies returned. His hand lingered on her forearm a few beats too long. This was it, the confirmation she was looking for. He *was* flirting.

Wasn't he?

No wonder you're single, Audrey. If Sabrina was here, she could tell you. Maybe he's just being a touchy-feely Sicilian.

Suddenly, she had a terrible thought. What if they put the two of them, together, in a single room? What if they expected her to sleep in a bed with Rafael? Her face blanched at the thought.

He must've sensed her unease, because he pulled away, almost too suddenly. "I should probably tell you a little about some of the people you'll be meet—" He stopped and took his foot off the gas. "We are almost there! First, a small stop. I'm low on gasoline."

They pulled into a small roadside station with a single old-style pump and a car service building with windows so dusted up, one could barely see the *APERTO* sign propped up in the corner. In America, this would be the kind of place she would've driven right past, in favor of a nice, clean Sunoco. She guessed that on this route, out practically in the

23

middle of nowhere, they didn't have much of a choice. This was actually one of the few busier intersections they'd come across.

"One moment. Can I get you anything to drink?" he asked her as he hopped out of the car.

She shook her head and spotted a tiny store on the corner, across the street, framed by a red plank fence and lots of unruly bushes and long grass. It looked like an abandoned place at first, but then Audrey noticed the faded sign in the dirty front picture window, and realized it was a junk store, with lots of dusty wares and rusting items for sale. Nothing of interest.

But that's when she saw it, among the old shovels, bird cages, auto parts, broken lawn equipment, and outdated furniture.

A beautiful antique mirror with a thick, leaden frame, embedded with multicolor glass stones.

Her jaw dropped. It was like finding a needle among a haystack, that beautiful, antique piece, waiting there, just for her. *That would be absolutely perfect in my upstairs bathroom!*

She lifted herself out of the car just as Rafael returned from inside and lifted the gas nozzle from the side of the pump. She said to him, "Do you mind if I go across the street to that store for a few minutes?"

"Oh, yes, a very nice antiques store. Not at all. Enjoy yourself. Do some shopping! Tell Maria and Flavio I said hello. They're the owners."

"Sure!" She grabbed her purse from the seat. Nick scratched at the door to his carrier, wanting to be let out. She leaned in and pressed her nose to his. "You'd cause too much trouble there, Bub. I'll be right back. Promise."

Hurrying across the empty road, as she came to the small wooden porch, she became even more excited. The glass was intact and a bit cloudy, though not too bad, much better than the broken thing she currently had. This mirror was a nice size, but what was best about the mirror was the iridescent stones inlaid in the thick lead frame. They sparkled in the bright sun, throwing prisms all over the porch. It was simply gorgeous. She could already picture it on the wall upstairs—it would be the showpiece of the bathroom, maybe even the entire house.

She stepped over an old manual lawn clipper and went past a bullet refrigerator that looked like it had seen better days, looking for the door of the store. She found it buried among knickknacks, from old jars and soup cans to giant carved columns that must've been rescued from old buildings.

She opened the screen door and went in, looking around as a bell overhead jingled. After that, the only sound was the whirring of a vacillating fan, which ruffled the pages of a giant pile of old magazines. Paintings on the walls of people from bygone eras stared back at her, all in mismatched frames of every shape. There wasn't a single open spot on the walls, and the floors weren't much better. Piles of unique things lay precariously perched in front of her like a pile of Jenga tiles. She had to wonder if one wrong move would create an avalanche.

Audrey thought she spotted a desk in the back of the room, so she tried to make her way over there, squeezing through the narrow path sideways. But when she got halfway there, a pillar blocked her way. She went back to the front door and tried again.

Looking down, careful not to take a wrong step, she nearly walked head-first into a stooped, bald old man. "Oh, I'm sorry!" she said, patting her chest in surprise. "Flavio?"

"Eh?" the man said, cupping his ear toward her.

She pointed. "*Scusami. Parli inglese?* I'm a friend of Rafael Piccolo. You know him? He said to tell you hi."

"Eh?"

Okay, this isn't going to be so easy. "I'm interested in a mirror outside. It's very beautiful. *Bella.* I wanted to purchase it? *Comprare?*"

The man's face scrunched up as she desperately tried to remember the Italian word for mirror. Instead, she drew a square, which only made him more confused. "Eh?"

She took a step toward the door and motioned for him to follow, hoping he'd catch her drift, but he only continued to stare at her.

Flustered, she brought out some of the Italian she'd learned. "*Vorrei comprare qualcosa . . .*" she said, but her accent was terrible. The poor old man probably had hearing loss, too. No wonder he couldn't understand.

She looked around, helpless, and was just about to go back to the car to get Rafael, when another man came in. He was built like a linebacker, with a beard and a loud-print shirt, open to reveal a lot of hair. Smiling at her, he said, "*Buongiorno, Flavio,*" then nodded politely at her. "*Buongiorno, signora.*"

"Oh. Excuse me. Do you speak English? *Scusami. Parli inglese?*"

"Yes. American, eh? You visit our corner of the world for tourism? What can I do for you?"

"Well, I'm trying to inform the shopkeeper that I'm interested in buying a piece outside."

"Ah. Bringing back a memento from Corleone, I see! Which piece?" His eyes sparkled. This man was clearly a lover of antiques.

"The mirror? But stupid me—I couldn't even remember the Sicilian word for mirror."

"Lo specchio."

"Oh, of course. Now I remember." She thumped the side of her head.

He nodded. "Yes, yes. The one with the stones? I saw it when I came in. Very lovely. I love the way it shines. You bring back to your home, eh, in America?"

She shook her head. "Not America. I live in Mussomeli. I'm renovating one of the one-dollar houses there. And I'd love to put the mirror in my bathroom, if it's not too expensive."

He nodded and began to speak to Flavio. Flavio nodded and together, the three of them went outside. The man helped Flavio pull the mirror free of the other junk around it. As they did, Audrey only became more certain that this was the right piece for her home.

"How much is it?" she asked as Flavio took a cloth and rubbed the layers of dust from it. *"Quanto costa?"*

Flavio rubbed his grizzled jaw, thinking. *"Cento."*

Audrey's eyes widened. She couldn't have heard him right. Or something had gotten lost in the translation. But then the other man said, "One hundred euros," confirming her original understanding.

"One hundred?" She clapped her hands. She'd expected it to be ten times that much. "Yes. Sold! It's mine. I'll take it."

The large, bearded man spoke to Flavio, who lifted the mirror and began to bring it inside. Audrey followed, rummaging through her purse for her cash. "I've been in Sicily five months and I still can't get the hang of the language. Not sure if I ever will. So thank you for translating, Mr. . . . I mean, *Signore. . .*"

"Capaldi. Marco Capaldi." He reached out his hand to shake hers. "And it is my pleasure to help you."

"Hi. I'm Audrey. Again, thanks. I can't tell you how much I appreciate it."

"No no. The pleasure is mine! We love our tourists here in Corleone. Unfortunately, we don't get very many."

"Probably because of the whole mafia thing," she blurted, and then cringed, horrified, when his face fell. What if he knew mafia people? What if he was mafia himself? She put down the money on the counter and lifted her mirror, which the old man had wrapped carefully in craft paper. *"Grazie!"*

When she hurried to the gas station, aware she'd taken far more time than she'd meant to take, Rafael was parked off to the side, drinking a cup of water. He handed one to her. "I know you said you did not want anything, but I thought you might be thirsty." Noticing her package, he climbed out of the car and helped her put it into the back. "You did some shopping? Get something good, did you?"

She nodded. "A beautiful antique mirror. I saw it and had to have it. I hope you don't mind that I took so long, and that I bought it? I should've asked if we had room . . . ?"

"Not at all. We have plenty of room. I am glad you found it. A beautiful mirror for a beautiful girl. I always find something interesting in Flavio's shop. He gets very nice things."

When they took off again, Audrey's spirits were a lot lighter. Coming to Corleone hadn't been all bad. If she hadn't been dragged on this trip, she never would've found the mirror. "So how far away is the Piccolo estate?" she asked. "It must be pretty big if there are going to be nearly one hundred people there."

He nodded. "Yes, quite big. But it is only just immediate family. Only six families in all. And it's right over this next hill. Which reminds me, I wanted to tell you . . . I have very many American relations. The Randazzos, you talk to them. Some of the Piccolos are okay, too. But I wouldn't talk to Uncle Mario. He doesn't like the Americans. Stay away from any of the Apontes. You understand?"

She blinked. "I did tell you I'm terrible with names, didn't?" she said, fear suddenly spiking in her. "What's wrong with the Apontes?"

He waved the notion away. "Don't worry. I will steer you in the right direction."

She stiffened. But what if he didn't? What if he left to use the restroom and an Aponte cornered her? Not for the first time, she couldn't help thinking she'd made a terrible mistake. What if this wasn't just a mistake . . . what if it was actually dangerous?

CHAPTER FIVE

They drove through the center of town and down a hill, past an old, crumbling church on the edge of town. Just when Audrey thought they were heading out into the middle of nowhere, Rafael turned onto a long gravel drive. There was a sign on a boulder beside it that said, *Cielo d'Azzurro.* She read it out loud.

Rafael nodded. "That's the name of our humble estate," he said, as they passed rows and rows of grapevines. "It means, of course, Blue Skies."

"A winery? I didn't know your family was involved in—"

"Oh yes. Wine, citrus. We do it all," he said with a charming smile. "It's been in our family for many generations."

They drove over hills and through groves of cypress trees and pines, and yet she didn't spot a house until several minutes later, when a sprawling stucco villa rose up in the distance, with a terra-cotta roof and arched porticos. The circular drive was choked with cars. Audrey counted more than a few Ferraris. She gasped as they pulled around a massive fountain which looked like a miniature Trevi Fountain, complete with golden statues of Roman gods.

"Wow," Audrey said, her mouth hanging open.

"A little overdone for my taste," he said with a shrug. "I prefer the simple family home in Mussomeli. But my grandfather was a man of distinguished tastes."

His villa outside Mussomeli was a mansion in its own right, far from simple. But Audrey supposed anyone who grew up in a monstrosity like the building before her would probably have a different outlook on life than most. This thing made the lifestyles of most Hollywood power-players look small.

"Signore Piccolo!" a man in a white waistcoat said, jogging down the marble staircase to them. He opened the door for Audrey and helped her out, then spoke Sicilian to Rafael in a low voice. Audrey could only make out a few words… *We have been waiting for you,* and something about *concern.*

Whatever it was, it clearly flustered the man, but Rafael brushed it off.

"Alfonzo, let me introduce you to Audrey," Rafael said, clapping the man on the back. "Audrey, this is Alfonzo. If there is anything you need during your stay, please see him first. He is the first, the best, the only man you need in your life. Except me, of course!"

He laughed heartily, and Alfonzo joined in. Audrey merely smiled. Was that flirting? Whatever it was, she couldn't help feeling like the butler was on edge about something as he reached in to grab Nick's case.

"Oh, I'll get that," she said, taking it. She set it on the hood of the car and opened the door to give Nick a little pet. "Don't worry, Nick. Let me just find a place to put you, and then you can—"

Before she could finish her sentence, he dashed past her, landing on the driveway and racing off into the manicured hedges.

"Nick!" she called, but he was already long gone. She stooped slightly to try to spot him, but he was nowhere in sight.

"Don't worry," Rafael said, coming up beside her. "I'm sure he'll be fine. He probably could taste the Piccolo grapes from here! He will be well-fed, that is for sure."

Audrey gnawed on her lip. Rafael was probably right. Nick never stayed in one place, and always liked to forage and have his own adventures, but he was never far away and usually showed up when she needed him. He'd likely be fine.

But something about it concerned her. Maybe it was being in a new, unfamiliar place, with untold dangers, or that it was supposedly mafia, but her stomach twisted.

She managed to forget her worries when he guided her upstairs and into a grand foyer, filled with even more Roman statues and rather gaudy décor—checkerboard tile floors and bright yellow walls, fake flowers and plants everywhere, and ivy climbing up a series of golden lattices around the circular entry room. It felt like the explosion of a sunset. And was that a miniature of David on a pedestal in the center of the foyer?

Before she could inspect it, Rafael took her arm and whisked her into a large parlor. She hardly had a chance to breathe before the introductions began. Suddenly, they were swarmed by Piccolos.

Rafael greeted them warmly with hugs and kisses, even the men. What Audrey hadn't expected was that even though they barely knew her, they'd do the same to her. Their squeezes were full-bodied, enthusiastic, nearly forcing the life out of her, and more than once, her cheeks felt wet from the saliva of someone's kiss, but she refrained from wiping them. Everyone was as loud and brash as the décor.

Rocco, one of Rafael's cousins whom she'd met earlier in Mussomeli, came up to her and gave her a hug that was so big, he actually lifted her up off the ground.

As she wrapped her arms around him, she felt it. A gun, strapped under his blazer.

After that, she stiffened, and noticed it on all the men. They were all carrying guns . . . to a family function.

Why? Wasn't it safe here, among family?

Was Rafael carrying one, too?

Maybe when you were mafia, no place was safe.

Forcing away the thought of a gangster-style shootout erupting in the middle of the home, she smiled along, trying to remember who it was that Rafael told her to stay away from. *Who was it? The Abruzzos? I can't remember.*

She leaned in to ask him, but he was too busy, conversing with a cousin. It didn't matter. He was right next to her, guiding her. He wouldn't lead her into trouble.

Someone gave them Bellinis, which she'd never had before but loved. Sweet and peachy, it went down like water. The laughter was loud, and everyone was in a good, partying mood. Most people spoke English, and they ribbed Rafael, telling jokes as if Audrey was in on it with them.

She had to admit, she liked this. Growing up, just the three of them—Audrey, her mom, Sabrina, they rarely had big parties. And she wasn't much for going out in high school and college, preferring to study instead. But this . . . this was actually . . . fun. They all paid attention to her, treating her like the woman of the hour.

After her second Bellini, her smile, while at first forced, became natural, and she forgot about the heat they were all packing.

As she stood there listening to his other cousins talk about some family trip they'd taken to Venice, a young woman with piles of bright red, over-styled hair and a face full of hot pink—hot pink lipstick, hot pink blush, and hot pink eyeshadow—came over to her. She was wearing skin-tight pants and a tank top.

"Hi. I'm Patty Randazzo, from *Nork*!" she said loudly, leaning in to give her a hug.

The woman smelled like too much perfume; it made Audrey's eyes water. "Oh! You're an American?"

The woman looked at her, surprised. "Yeah. I'm from Nork. Like I said."

"Nork? Where is that?"

She giggled. "Oh. Sorry. *New-ark*."

"Oh! Newark, New Jersey. Right? Or Dela—"

"Come on! There really is only one *Nork*! Am I right?" She bumped her playfully with her hip. "So. Rafael just told me about you. Audrey, right? You're a veterinarian, right? From Boston?"

She pronounced her name with a deep, emphasized *aw* sound. *Awd-rey*. Audrey didn't mind it. She was happy to have someone from America, who she didn't have to try to stumble though her conversation with. That was probably why she liked Mason so much—it made life so much easier, to not have to worry about the language barrier.

Although, she had *other* barriers when it came to him.

"Yes, that's me. Are you related to Rafael?"

She snapped her gum. "Oh, sure. He's my third cousin, twice removed. On my father's side. We go way back, though he is a decade older than me. Listen, *Awd*," she said, lifting up her small purse. "I was wondering if you could take a look at my Pickle here."

Audrey's eyes narrowed in confusion. "Your—"

"He's right here in my pocketbook." She opened the flap to reveal the tiniest of teacup chihuahuas. "I got him six weeks ago. Pickle doesn't go anywhere without me, right, Pickle Poo?"

The dog, barely a handful, gazed up at them with the saddest eyes as the woman scooped him into her arms. "What seems to be the problem?"

"Well, he won't eat a darn thing. He just wants to lie there like a lazybones. I get the feeling he's under the weather."

But Audrey could tell right away that the problem was much bigger than that. As she took the animal into her hands, it was lifeless and limp.

She hadn't planned on catering to any animals this weekend, but instantly, her senses kicked into overdrive, and she knew exactly what was wrong.

Looking around, she spotted the bar at the corner of the vast room and began to make her way over to it. Maybe fate had brought her here for a reason, because now there wasn't a moment to lose.

CHAPTER SIX

"Hypoglycemia," Audrey explained as she held the shivering pup in her arms and syringe-fed him more sugar water. Pickle was now more alert, his eyes more awake and brighter. "It's very common with very tiny animals when they skip a meal or two. It's important to keep them on a stringent feeding schedule. When was the last time he ate?"

"Well, I was on the plane, talking to the handsomest doctor, you know . . ." Patty said, shaking her head. "I guess I forgot to feed him."

A small group of interested Piccolos had gathered around her to watch. Luckily, some simple table sugar dissolved in water, and some careful feeding, plus a blanket to keep the poor creature warm, seemed to do the trick. He finished lapping up the water and yipped happily.

The crowd around her seemed to be holding its breath, but when she smiled, they burst into applause and rowdy cheers. People patted her on the back. Audrey didn't think she'd have gotten a better response if she'd done a magic track.

As Audrey handed Pickle back to Patty, Patty said, "You're a miracle worker, truly. What do I owe you?"

"Oh, nothing. Really, it's on me," Audrey said with a smile. "Just remember that teacup breeds are very fragile. They can't skip meals. Do you have some food on you?"

Patty nodded. "In the kitchen. I'll get it right away. You think you can help? I'm not sure how much to feed."

"Sure." Audrey followed her into a massive gourmet kitchen with a center island that was bigger than Audrey's entire kitchen in Mussomeli. There was an industrial-sized refrigerator, double convection ovens, and plenty more gaudy artwork—there was a trellis painted on a wall, with grapevines everywhere. Dozens of servants ran about like it was Grand Central Station, preparing and delivering food and drink. They seemed to part to let Patty go past, as if she were someone important, or someone they were afraid of. Audrey couldn't tell which.

Audrey approved of the dog food she'd chosen. It was a good brand for the breed. She showed Patty exactly how much to feed the pup. "Most dogs only eat once a day, but little dogs like this eat two to three

32

times a day, more if they're puppies. Start with a quarter cup and see where that gets him." She set it down on the placemat in a quiet corner of the kitchen, and Pickle went right for it. "That should do it."

Patty patted her heart and batted her long, thickly coated lashes. "You saved my life. You really did. I don't know what I'd have done if something happened to him." She latched onto Audrey's arm. "So, when you get back into the States, we should hang out. Ever been to the clubs in downtown Hoboken? They're the *best*."

"Well, I'm probably not going back to the States anytime soon. At least, I don't think so. I'm fixing up a house in Sicily, to hopefully live in, for now."

She squealed. "Really? Mussomeli, right? That's how you met Rafael?"

"That's right."

"I've heard that villa out there is sweet! He keeps telling me Bruno and I should take the ride over. I'd love to come visit!"

Audrey gritted her teeth. "Uh, sure," she said, hoping that was one of those things that people said they'd do on vacation, but never got around to following up on. After all, she'd be going back to America soon. "I'm sure you'll be busy, though, during your time here, and Mussomeli is a small town. There's not really all that much to do . . ."

"That's okay! I have gads of time! I'm here for the rest of the year, actually. I stay here with Uncle Carmine on the weekends, while at the University of Palermo."

"Oh. You're in school?"

She popped her gum. "No. I live with my boyfriend, Bruno. He's a cleaning guy there. But only during the week. He's so busy on the weekends, so there's nothing to do there."

"Oh . . . um, so, Uncle Carmine, he's. . . you mean . . ."

She looked at Audrey like she had three heads. "Carmine. Rafael's dad. The big guy. Well, technically not until his father croaks, but have you seen the old man? He's not doing so well. They had to admit him to a nursing home this morning."

"Oh, no! Really? Does Rafael know?"

"He just found out. But it's better for everyone that way. Old guy was drooling, insane . . . had no idea where he was. Did you see him?"

"Yes, as a matter of fact, I met him in Mussomeli. I feel terrible that he's doing so badly now. He seemed frail the last time I saw him, but . . . for him to miss this? How sad!"

"Yeah. It's awful," she muttered, snapping her gum. "So Carmine pretty much handles all the business. He's . . ." She made a face. "Interesting."

"What does that mean?"

"You know how Rafael is sweet and personable?"

She nodded. Well, Rafael had been very intimidating, the first time she met him. But she'd warmed up to him a bit. "Carmine is not?"

"Oh, he can be. If he knows you. Respects you. If not . . . watch out. He's been known to tear a few heads off."

Now Audrey made the same sick face.

Patty rubbed Audrey's shoulder. "Don't worry. Knowing Rafael, he already put in a good word for you." She looked up. "Speak of the devil."

Audrey looked up to find Rafael crossing the kitchen toward them. He said, "I was wondering where you escaped to." He leaned in and kissed Patty's cheek. "Patricia, you are looking wonderful, as always. Last time I saw you, you were but a teenager."

She giggled. "Rafe, you're looking really good. No wonder you've got yourself such a smart girlfriend."

This is it. Audrey swung to look at him, waiting for him to either decline that they were dating, or affirm it.

"Thank you, cousin," he said. *Or just ignore the comment altogether.* She waited for him to look at her and squeeze her hand, or something. Instead, his eyes trailed to Pickle. "The house is all abuzz with some miracle you performed, Audrey. Is it true?"

"It was nothing," Audrey said. "Really. The puppy just needed some nourishment."

"Nothing? We Sicilians are very protective of our pets," he said, stooping to pet the pup. "You must know that by now, working in Mussomeli. They are not just our pets, they are our family. So when you offer assistance to one of them, it is no small favor."

Patty nodded seriously. "Very true, cousin. If she hadn't been here, I'm afraid poor Pickle would be done for."

He took Audrey's free arm and smiled at Patty. "You mind if I take her from you? I have some more people to introduce her to."

Patty's face fell. "I suppose. But bring her back! I'm planning to visit youse guys in Mussomeli! And then she and I are going to meet up in Hoboken!" As Rafael tugged Audrey away, Patty called after them, "Bye, best friend! Don't forget!"

Rafael leaned into Audrey, his warm breath tickling her ear. "I apologize for leaving you alone with her. Some of my relatives can be a bit . . . overbearing, in case you didn't notice."

"They're fine. And she was very nice," Audrey said. Even if they had been annoying, she wasn't about to tell him that. After all . . . mafia.

"You're too understanding," he said, entwining his fingers with her own. "Come. I will introduce you to the most important person here, besides yourself."

She stiffened. "Your father?"

He nodded, then looked back at her. "Do not be afraid. He will love you." He leaned closer. "He loves all the pretty girls. My mama, God rest her soul, has been gone some twenty years, and though he remains faithful to her in spirit, he has always had an eye for a pretty woman."

"Great," she said bitterly, then bit her tongue. She hadn't meant to say that aloud. But the last thing she needed was to catch the eye of Carmine Piccolo.

"Don't you go falling for his charms, though," he said with a wink as they went through the crowd, into a masculine office, which was all dark mahogany and old, flowered wallpaper. Men in dark suits were all crowded at one end around a man at the desk, who was smoking a cigar. It looked like he was holding court.

They even had to wait in line for their turn. As they did, Audrey peered over the shoulders of the people in front of her to see a handsome man who didn't look much older than Rafael. He looked far younger and slimmer than the Marlon Brando character she'd been expecting, though he was decked out in the same dark suit. He motioned to a man behind him, who leaned in. Carmine whispered something, then uninterestedly motioned the people in front of Audrey away.

They departed, leaving Rafael and Audrey at the front of the line.

It felt like she was open to attack as they stepped up to meet him. The Bellini she'd imbibed earlier did nothing to calm her nerves. In fact, she felt like it was trying to force its way back up her throat.

Carmine Piccolo gave them an icy, indifferent glare. "Rafael."

The word, deep and raspy, hung in the air for what felt like an eternity.

"Father," Rafael said, lunging forward desperately and kissing his father's ring.

Well, that's a tad dramatic, Audrey thought as the man motioned his son away with a flick of a manicured hand.

She thought of her relationship with her own father. As strange as it was that he'd left her at age twelve, never to be heard from again. . . their relationship didn't seem as twisted as this one.

Rafael backed up quickly, as instructed, thrust an arm behind Audrey, and tried to guide her forward. But Audrey felt rooted to the spot. The man was staring at her. The *godfather* was staring at her. She momentarily forgot how to breathe.

Rafael applied more pressure to her back, until her balance could take it no longer, and she went stumbling forward. She caught herself by putting her hands on the glossy surface of the desk. His eyes, still full of ice, dropped to her hands. She quickly snatched them off the desk, leaving fingerprints.

"Uh, hi," she peeped. "Sorry."

"This is Audrey, from America," Rafael said, pausing for his father's approval. The silence was painful. When nothing came, he added, "She's my date for this weekend."

Carmine ran an eye over her and said, in a guttural voice, "I hear you are the one who did something with a dog?"

Did something? That was rather vague. From his tone, she couldn't tell whether he was pleased or upset by what she'd done. She nodded. "I treated Pickle. I'm a vet. Yes."

He tented his fingers together on the desk. "I don't like that little mongrel. But my niece does. She is in your debt, no doubt."

Audrey shook her head. Apparently, debts were big things among this family. "No, it was nothing, real—"

He snapped his fingers and one of the men standing behind him bent down to listen. "My grand-nephew Leo will give you a small token of our appreciation."

Oh, god. It's a horse head. She waved her hands. "Oh, no, really—"

The younger man handed her a velvet jewel case. She stared at it. It looked like a box for an engagement ring.

Oh, god. That's even worse . . .

"Open it," Rafael said, leaning over her excitedly.

"Okay," she said tentatively. She glanced at him as she did, praying that he wouldn't drop to one knee beside her.

36

But then she realized it was simply a gold coin with what looked like a picture of an old man, in profile, on it. "It's our family coin," the don said proudly.

Her stomach swam. She knew that in the mafia, gifts were a form of extortion. Oranges from Rafael were one thing, but this? This was big-time, from the don himself. If she accepted the gift, he might call in that "favor" in the future, and who knew what that would entail? But a refusal would show lack of respect. It would be seen as an insult.

No matter what she did, she was in trouble.

But a motto was already forming in her head, one that she felt compelled to obey: *Never say no to the mafia.*

So she did the only thing she could do. "Thank you. It's lovely."

"My son Rafael is quite taken with you," the don said. "You might be the one to change him."

She paused and looked over at Rafael, who for once looked a little uncomfortable. Her thoughts once again turned to that white machine-gun wedding. "Change him? Oh, he doesn't need changing . . ." *Was that saying no to the mafia?* "I mean, he's so great, as he is."

"And yet, I think you might make him into a better man."

Her friends and family back home would just love hearing about that one. *Guess what, Sabrina? I'm married now . . . to the mob. And that means, so are you.*

"Well, that's nice. I think he's . . ." She paused, wondering how to phrase it so that they wouldn't think she wanted to marry him. "Great, too. Really a great guy. A good *friend.*"

She punched Rafael on the arm, as if to say, *Hey, ol' pal.*

Carmine studied her curiously for a long time, until she was sure she'd done something wrong. So she added, "But we'll see what happens. These things take time."

More time than just a weekend. If I come back to Mussomeli married to the Piccolos, what will Mason say?

She thought Carmine might argue. But instead, he said, "I am pleased to meet you, glad to have you here in our humble home as a guest. Please make yourself comfortable."

She let out a breath of relief. Next to her, Rafael said, "Thank you. Thank you, *padre*," and kissed both of his hands this time.

As she wondered if she should do the same, Carmine said, "I have business to attend to, now. Please leave us."

Audrey followed Rafael out, feeling like the noose around her neck had been loosened ever so slightly. He wasn't the grim reaper, but he wasn't the romantic charmer she'd been expecting either. When she reached the lobby and could breathe again, she was surprised to find her clothing damp from sweating. She felt like she'd run a mile in hundred-degree heat.

When they were out in the living area, Rafael turned to her, a serious expression on his face. "You are very fortunate. Very few people get the Piccolo coin."

The velvet of the case in her palm was now damp because of her perspiration. "I feel very fortunate," she said, even though she didn't. It felt like it was burning a hole there, like one day, she might regret having it.

"Come, now," he said, guiding her through the living area toward the back of the house. "More people to meet. And let me get you another Bellini."

CHAPTER SEVEN

Outside was a beautiful oasis with an inground pool, and gardens with flowers blooming everywhere. They walked to the lawn, where there were wooden chairs set up, and more people were playing lawn games. "Over there is the garden labyrinth. There's a secret fountain in the center. Maybe you would like to walk it?"

"Will we find our way out?" she asked, only half-joking.

He laughed. "I assure you, it's for contemplation of beauty. Not to confuse anyone." Rafael sat her on one of the chairs and said, "Will you be all right here alone? I'll get you that Bellini."

She laughed. He was so overly protective of her, she had to wonder if he really was concerned about someone from the family attacking her. "Thank you. I will be fine."

She leaned back, donned her sunglasses, and watched men—all dressed in suits—play a rousing game of bocce. They were really getting into it, razzing each other and egging other players on, cheering and booing loudly every time someone threw a ball too close or too far from the little ball.

When the game ended, a handsome, tanned, and slim young man scooped up the little ball and stooped next to her. "Want to get in on the next game, *bella*?"

She shook her head. "I've never played."

"Oh, it's easy. You can't do it wrong. Come. I teach you."

Shrugging, she stood up and followed him to the green. As she did, he leaned in, a little too close to her ear, and his breath tickled her skin as he whispered, "You are Audrey, the *veterinaria*? *Si*? You come with Rafael."

"I guess my reputation really does precede me!" she laughed, wondering if everyone there already knew her. "Who are you?"

"I am Alessandro, Rafael's little brother," he said with a wink. "Of course Rafi has not introduced you to me because he knows I am the most handsome of us. He is afraid I will whisk you away from his incredibly boring company."

She laughed. Despite his five o'clock shadow, he was wiry and had a baby face. She wasn't even sure the man was legal. "I doubt it. Rafael and I are just friends. So I am sure he would not mind either way. Me, on the other hand . . ."

"Hmm," he said, in a way that made her think he knew something she didn't. He held up the small ball. "Well, the weekend is young. Let me see what I can do to change your mind. This is the *pallino*. It's thrown first. Then, with the bocce balls, all you need to do is get as close as possible. I show you."

He threw the smaller ball on the lawn, and then followed with a bigger one. His first shot, and the two balls were only inches apart from one another. He was good at this.

"Now you try."

The ball was surprisingly heavy as she held it in her hand. He came behind her, pressing up unnaturally close to her, and held her hand, trying to guide her. His aftershave was so overwhelming, her eyes teared. She stiffened and looked at him. "Uh. Do you mind? I can do this myself."

He backed off a little, grinning wolfishly. "*Scuzi*. But you smell *amazing*."

Was that his way of trying to distract her so she misfired? She waved him away. She pulled back, underhanded, and let it go. She let out a little squeal as the ball hit the *pallino*, pushing it along a bit before coming to rest right next to it. "Is that good?"

He nodded and touched her arm flirtatiously. "Very, sweet girl. You can be on my team. We can be the sexy ones, *si*?"

Then he tossed the next ball and knocked her ball far away. She frowned. "What did you just do?"

"Aw, don't be sad, *bella*." He reached out and pushed a lock of her hair behind her ear. "That's the way the game is played. You win some, you lose some."

"Bleh," she said, as she spotted a reddish form near the bushes on the outskirts of the property. She squinted in the fading sunlight. Was it just the shadows playing tricks on her, or was that who she thought it was? When it moved, her suspicions were confirmed. "Nick!"

She broke into a run.

"Who is Nick? Another man I need to pull you away from?" Alessandro called, then took off after her.

She stopped at the edge of the line of bushes, where she'd last seen him, and looked up and down the line of shrubbery. No Nick. "Meh. I thought I saw my pet here. I lost him."

"I didn't see anything. Just a fox."

"*That's* Nick," she told him.

His eyes widened. "Oh. Well, I think he's gone now. He ran into those trees."

"I hope he doesn't get lost," she said, twisting her hands. "He's not familiar with these grounds."

He grabbed one of her hands suddenly and smiled. "If this was your way of getting me alone, it worked. Shall we go into the woods? I know a place where we can be *very* alone . . ." He licked his lips and leaned in to nuzzle her neck.

Before she could even think to swat him away, Rafael arrived.

She nudged him. "*No*," she said firmly. She would've smacked him, but . . . mafia.

She blushed, thinking she'd have to explain why the two of them were out here alone, and with him whispering sweet nothings into her ear, but Rafael didn't seem upset in the least.

As he handed her the Bellini, he said, "I see my little brother is trying to use his charms on you, taking you all the way out here into the woods. You must watch him. He is a scoundrel."

"Oh, no. I just came here because I thought I saw Nick."

"Did you, now?"

"Yes. But he ran off."

Rafael motioned his brother off. "Sandro. *Andare.*"

The kid winked at her and scurried off. Audrey sipped her drink. "He was just showing me how to play bocce before that."

"With that boy, there is no *just* anything. He is fourteen years my junior and twice the rascal I ever was. I've lost track of all of his girlfriends." He smiled and looked out upon the grounds. "Come. Let's walk through the gardens and the labyrinth. I will guide you through and show you how easy it is."

He put his arm out to her, and she took it. As she did, her hand swiped something hard underneath his blazer.

A gun.

So that answered *that* question.

But at least Rafael was a friend. The others, she wasn't sure about. If anyone was going to have a gun around her, she was glad it was someone who she knew was protective of her.

They walked among the rosebushes, fountains, and Roman statues, with vines and hedges so overgrown that they created a shady canopy overhead. Every once in a while, Rafael would stop and tell her about a flower he liked, or a place where something important had happened.

41

"There's the corner of the fountain where Sandro fell and cut his head open when he was twelve. There's the bench where my father proposed to my mother, forty years ago."

She sipped her Bellini, taking it all in and enjoying his company. "It must've been interesting, growing up with your father. Do you have any siblings besides Alessandro?"

"No."

"You and your father seemed rather distant, which was odd, considering you're the heir of his dynasty."

"Oh, no. We're very close. But—"

"But he's a very important man. Has a lot on his mind?"

He nodded. "It's not just that. He tried to be there all the time while we were growing up. He was a doting father, believe me. But I've done things—things that I know have disappointed him. That he disapproves of. And so our relationship is rather strained, unfortunately." He cleared his throat. "Sometimes, I—"

She looked at him, but he shook his head.

"Nothing," he said, and patted her hand.

They rounded a corner and bumped into Patty, who was out walking Pickle. "Hi!" she said, waving at them. "He's much better now."

"He looks it," Audrey remarked, bending down to scratch his ears.

"Yes, I thought I'd just take my little Pickle Poo out here to do a tinkle before dinner and Bruno gets here," she explained, checking her cell phone. "Which reminds me, my boyfriend should be here any moment! He was working late at the school, cleaning up after some event, but he should've been here by now."

"Luigi bringing him?" Rafael asked.

Patty nodded. "Probably got caught in traffic, knowing him. I can't wait for you to meet him, Audrey!"

"I can't wait to meet him, too," she said as they continued past. "I hope at dinner!"

"Yes!" Patty called after her. "I hope they sit us next to each other!"

When they were alone, Audrey whispered, "There are assigned seats?"

"Always. It's to keep family that might not get along so well from creating any problems." Before she could ask what *problems*, exactly, and whether they involved guns, Rafael shrugged and said, "You are very kind to Patty. I appreciate that. She can be a bit much, but she has a good heart. She is one of my favorite cousins, and I have over a hundred of them. Not all of them are here, of course. They are scattered across the world."

"Wow," Audrey said, as a strange sound filled the air. It sounded like someone was blowing a horn to summon a wild animal.

Rafael laughed at the confused expression on her face and said, "That is my family's way of announcing dinner is served." He extended a hooked arm to her. "Shall we go in?"

She took it once again, and again, she brushed the butt of his gun with her knuckles. Sucking in a breath, she tried to ignore it. "So tell me, Rafael . . . What are these flowers called?"

*

There was a large tent set out on the lawn, behind the giant swimming pool. Audrey understood why they'd gone through such trouble when she saw how many people were inside the tent. The table was enormous, practically the size of the pool itself.

Most people were already seated. Rafael led her around the perimeter of the tent, stopping at two chairs. "Here we are. Audrey Smart and Rafael." He lifted a tiny frame to show her. "We're sitting together."

"I should hope so!" she said as she sat down beside a rather large older man. She recognized him. It was Blocko, from Mussomeli. "I know you!"

He nodded and shifted in his chair. "Franco. Rafael's cousin." He shook her hand. "*Dottore* Smart. Nice to see you again."

"Franco is a Randazzo. He is Patty's great-uncle," Rafael explained, leaning in as a man in a white coat came around, filling champagne glasses.

Audrey nodded, wishing she had a family tree to consult.

He started to continue speaking, when there was the sudden clinking of silverware against crystal. Audrey turned with everyone else toward the head of the table, where Carmine stood, flanked by other enormous men that must've been his bodyguards.

He spoke loudly and authoritatively. "Oh, my friends, my family. It is a rare but joyous time that we can all be together. First, Padre Mario will lead us in prayer."

It was only then that Audrey noticed the man a few seats down from Carmine, wearing a full priest's cassock and collar. He stood up and crossed himself, as did most everyone around the table, and said,

43

"Benedici, Signore, noi e questi tuoi doni, che stiamo per ricevere dalla tua generosità. Per Cristo nostro Signore."

Audrey bowed politely, and they crossed themselves again and said, "Amen."

The don continued. "I am so happy to be with you all. So happy, words cannot express it. I have love for each of you, and you all have my greatest respect and admiration, for as long as I shall live." He lifted his glass. "To *la famiglia!*"

"To *la famiglia!*" everyone roared back, and applauded wildly.

Audrey looked past Rafael and noticed two empty chairs. As she was about to ask who was missing, she noted the placard. *Patricia.*

She was about to ask where Patty had gone off to when the girl arrived, cradling Pickle in her arms. Her cheeks were even more pink than usual, and she seemed rather flustered. "Oh, Bruno's still not here. I tried texting him. No answer. He's probably on the road."

Rafael pulled out a chair for her. "Don't worry, Patty. He'll be here."

"I don't want your father getting upset," she said with a cautious glance in his direction.

"You're fine," he told her, then whispered something in Sicilian to her. Audrey wished she could make it out, but Patty simply nodded and whispered back, *"Grazie."*

They settled in, and moments later, white-coated servants arrived with plates of *antipasti*, salads full of cured meats, black olives, artichokes, provolone, roasted red peppers, and mushrooms, all drenched in oil and vinegar. It was only when the plate was placed in front of her that Audrey realized how hungry she was.

"This looks delicious," she said, digging in.

Patty smiled. "Wait until you have Uncle Carmine's pasta. He makes it himself."

"He does?" Audrey asked with a raised eyebrow, looking at Rafael for confirmation. She couldn't see the powerful don rolling out dough in the kitchen, complete with frilly apron.

"It's true," Rafael said, placing his napkin on his lap. "He takes great care in making sure each strand of his pasta is perfect. He lays it out, piece by piece, all over the kitchen. It's the best you'll ever taste."

She licked her lips and picked up her fork. "Can't wait."

Soft music played from a band stationed in the corner, but it was barely noticeable above the roar of lively conversation all around. As she ate, she took in the members of the family all around her. Despite the careful placement of the nameplates, it seemed as though arguments were breaking out all over. Audrey wasn't sure—since it was all in Sicilian, maybe they were just conversing passionately. That was one thing these people didn't lack—passion.

"Are you enjoying yourself?" Rafael asked as he handed her a basket of fresh bread to pass around.

"Oh, yes. This is a very nice meal," she said, hardly able to hear her own voice over the competing loud voices and the band. "So much food! Do you eat like this all the time?"

He patted his stomach. "No. If I did, I think I'd be in trouble. Is the champagne to your liking? We grow the grapes here. *Spumante Brut.* This is our family label."

"It's absolutely delicious," she said, as a waiter reached over and refilled her glass. She wasn't used to drinking more than a couple alcoholic beverages a night. Much more of that, and she wouldn't be able to walk. *I need to pace myself,* she warned herself.

"Good." He reached over and squeezed her hand. "I hope that—"

His voice was interrupted by a loud scream.

Heads swung in the direction of the tent's opening. People shifted suddenly, and then somehow, oddly, things came to a halt. Everything seemed frozen in time. Mouths opened wide, some still full of antipasti. Some people were still holding their champagne glasses, even as the band's lively song came to a stop, like a skipped recording.

Audrey could feel it at once. Something was wrong, and yet she didn't know quite what.

But the other people around the table seemed to, almost as if they'd expected it.

Rafael reached underneath his blazer for his gun and jumped to standing, blocking her way. Leaning forward to see around him and discover what the commotion was, Audrey barely had time to register the two men standing in the tent opening, before realizing they weren't holding trays of food.

They were bleeding.

The men staggered toward the table, but that was the last thing she saw before a strong hand pushed her back to her seat, and Patty shouted, "Oh my *gawd*! There's a shooter outside!"

45

CHAPTER EIGHT

Screaming. That was all she heard.

At first, she thought it was Patty, who was crouching behind her on her chair, hugging herself as everyone jumped up to see what was the matter.

Then she realized it was herself.

Chaos ensued. She whipped her head around, trying to understand what everyone was saying. Wondering if she should dive underneath the table to avoid the gunshots. But she didn't hear any gunshots. Maybe in her terror, her ears ceased to work the right way.

When she looked up, Rafael was stooping down over her, wiping her hair from her face. His expression was full of concern. "Audrey?"

Stunned, she couldn't bring herself to answer.

"Do not go anywhere. I will be right back!" he commanded, rising to his feet and running off.

Audrey did as she was told, staring up at the slowly spinning ceiling fan above her. The ground echoed with the sound of people running. Her entire body was shaking. Screams seemed to echo around her, faraway, along with the incessant yipping of Pickle, somewhere . . .

It seemed like hours before she got up the courage to sit up and look around. By then, she was able to make sense of the voices. They were screaming, *Dottore.*

Doctor. I'm a doctor.

Pushing onto her elbows, she took in the chaotic scene around her. "Is there a shooter somewhere?" she asked, but her question fell into a void.

People were running everywhere. Still no gunshots. Most of the men had fled, probably chasing after the shooters. When Audrey saw a body lying on the floor, on its side, motionless but facing away from her, surrounded by confused people, it suddenly hit her: *You're probably the only doctor here.*

Rolling onto her hands and knees, she crawled over to the person, through the crowd, and said, "I'm a doctor!"

The group parted. She stumbled to the body and assessed the situation. It was a young man, and he'd taken a bullet to the arm. He was calm, but wincing slightly, his eyes darting about, unfocused.

"Hey. Look at me," she said calmly. Nudging off his jacket, she worked to unbutton his shirt. When she pulled it off, she sighed in relief. It wasn't too terrible; the bullet had only grazed the flesh of his arm. She could handle this.

Even so, it was bleeding terribly. She reached up and grabbed a couple of napkins as someone nudged her from behind.

It was Patty. "Pickle! Pickle Poo! Here, boy!" she was shouting. "Did you see Pickle?"

"I heard him, but haven't seen him. He probably ran off when he heard the commotion. Is there a shooter somewhere?"

"I don't know! I just saw all of that *blood*!" Patty groused, looking around. "Well, this is just—PICKLE! Get your scrawny little tail over here before someone steps on you!"

"*Aiuto! Qualcuno aiuti!*" someone shouted across the table.

Audrey knew the word for "help" when she heard it. She straightened her back and peered over the table to see a woman crying desperately.

"Aunt Angela! What is wrong?" Patty shouted across the table at the woman, who continued to sob. Patty rolled her eyes. "Aunt Angela's a bit of a dramatic, if you know what I mean."

Audrey let out a huff of a breath. As far as she was concerned, Aunt Angela was well within her rights to be freaking out at this moment. Someone had just opened fire on them!

I have to get over there and see what's going on, Audrey thought.

"Can you help me?" Audrey asked Patty, wrapping Franco's arm quickly in one of the linen napkins. She tied it tight, but it was bleeding through. She gave Patty the other napkin. "Take this and help him hold his arm like this. Apply pressure. Okay?"

Patty nodded and did as she was told.

Audrey pulled away from him and quickly made her way around the table. As she did, she took in the scene. Mostly older men and women were sitting about, looking like the survivors of a long battle.

But there was also something eerie about the scene, and strangely less chaotic than she'd seen in news reports of mass shootings. Probably because these people weren't innocents so much as fighters in a war—casualties were expected. These people must've been used to gunshot wounds, because they seemed to have it rather under control.

"Who was the shooter?" she asked, hoping someone would understand.

Again, no answer.

It was only when she rounded the corner of the other side of the table and stood next to the crying woman, Aunt Angela, that Audrey saw what had worked the woman into such a state.

At first, she thought it was Rocco, the refrigerator-sized young man that she'd met in Mussomeli last month, one of Rafael's cousins. But then she realized it was a young man she'd never seen before.

There was a bright red flower of blood blooming and stretching over his white dress shirt. His eyes were full of fear, his breathing erratic.

Audrey dropped to her knees in a hurry, working to clear away his clothing so she could get a better look at the wound. As she did, he lunged forward and grabbed both of her wrists in such a hurry that she gasped.

"Non mi aspettavo questo . . ." he whispered frantically, choking on the words. *"Non mi . . ."*

Audrey struggled desperately to understand. *I didn't know . . . I didn't want . . .* She wasn't sure. "What is he saying?" she begged anyone who would listen.

But the woman behind her kept sobbing. Everyone else looked on, already mourning him, as if they knew there was no hope. No one answered her.

His voice was growing fainter as he locked eyes with her, silently begging for her to understand, to carry out his last wishes.

"I don't know what you're saying!" she cried, wishing she'd paid more attention to the lessons she listened to every night before she went to sleep. "Please . . ."

He closed his eyes, and for a moment she thought she'd lost him. But then his long eyelashes fluttered open, and he tried again. He pointed to the table. *"Fiori."*

Fiori. She knew that word. "Flowers?" she said, looking up at the table. Sure enough, there was a gorgeous arrangement of flowers at the very center, though now, it had been tipped over in the commotion. "What about them?"

He sputtered.

She leaned closer. "What about the flowers? What are you trying to say?"

But his eyes closed, and he went limp in her hands. His breathing slowed, and finally stopped.

Audrey stared at him, then checked for his pulse. But it was gone. She'd lost patients before, but this was the first time her patient had been human. Straightening, stunned, she looked at the sobbing people around her, the stone-faced men, and then back at the centerpiece.

Fiori. Flowers. What exactly about the flowers was he trying to convey?

Patty came by a moment later, cradling Pickle in her arms.

"Oh, no! Bruno!" she murmured, dropping to her knees. "Bruno! Speak to me."

"Bruno . . . your boyfriend?" Audrey covered her mouth with her hand. "Oh, God, Patty. I'm sorry. He's . . . he's dead."

In a scene that seemed right out of a mafia movie, Patty dropped Pickle to the ground and draped herself over her boyfriend's body.

Then she grabbed his lapels and shook him hard. "You stupid! Why didn't you come here when you said you were going to!" She rolled her eyes as she wiped tears from them. "It was his own fault. He never listened to me when I told him he should stay out of the family business. And now look at him!"

She threw his body down and scowled at him.

Then she looked up at Audrey expectantly. "Did he ask for me in his last moments, at least?"

Audrey cringed. "Well . . ."

"Of course he didn't." Her lips twisted. "Jerk."

Still reeling, Audrey stood up and looked around. Where was Rafael, anyway? She looked at Patty. The last thing she wanted to do was lose another patient. Not tonight. "What happened to Luigi?"

"Oh. He's with Leo," she said, slumping into her chair. "So much for a nice dinner. Once again, Bruno ruins everything."

Audrey backed away to let the poor old lady cry over the body.

Patty leaned over and patted her arm. "That's okay, Aunt Angela. Bruno's in a better place."

Audrey frowned. "He said something about flowers."

"Flowers?" Patty gave her a quizzical look. "Oh. He always liked flowers. Especially roses, like those. They were at his father's funeral. Of course, we always have red roses everywhere. They're kind of like the Piccolo family flower."

"I think he was trying to say something about them, though. But I don't know what."

Patty nodded. "Yeah. Bruno was always kind of *particular* about things. Liked things just so, if you know what I mean. Probably wanted to make sure we didn't screw up the funeral arrangements."

Audrey looked at her doubtfully. "Seriously?"

She nodded. "Sicilians have gone to war in this family over messed-up funeral arrangements. My grandmother nearly strangled the funeral director for putting yellow roses out instead of white. God rest their souls." She crossed herself and then blew a giant bubble with her gum.

Audrey couldn't believe she was talking in such a blasé fashion about her own boyfriend, who'd been murdered not minutes ago, whose dead body was still lying on the ground. Something told Audrey she'd seen a *lot* of murdered family members.

She surveyed the rest of the place, making sure everyone was all right.

It was only then, when she exhaled, that she looked down at her hands and realized she was shaking. Her hands were covered in blood, too. Her knees felt weak. She needed another glass of champagne to calm herself.

Patty noticed and sprang up. "Hey. Here. Sit down," she said, lowering Audrey into her chair and fanning her slightly. She grabbed a glass of water from one of the place settings. "Drink this."

Audrey took a sip. "Thanks. I feel better now. Where is Rafael?" she asked.

Patty looked around. "Oh. I don't know. Luigi said that the shooting happened in town. But I think the men went out after the shooters, to see if they could exact their revenge right away. *Men.* They can never just leave things be." She winced. "They'll probably shoot each other up."

Audrey swallowed. Revenge? What were they doing? And why did this sound like she'd just walked herself right into the middle of a mob war? "Are you serious?"

Patty pointed outside. "Which reminds me. . . we should probably check outside the tent and make sure no one else is hurt."

Audrey jumped up. She had a feeling her work here was not done.

CHAPTER NINE

Audrey rushed to the opening in the tent, her heels getting caught in the soft earth as she ran. When she reached the exit, Rafael came in, along with some of the other men. They all looked defeated as they opened their blazers and returned their guns to their shoulder holsters.

"Well?" Carmine demanded, as the crowd parted for him to approach his son. His jacket was off, and there was a sheen of sweat on his broad forehead, his face ruddy and full of rancor.

He shook his head. "We drove to town, but nothing. They got away."

Carmine threw up his hands and began to shout in Sicilian. Whatever it was, the longer it went on, the more wounded Rafael looked. Then the don wrapped a hand around the back of his son's neck and brought him close to his face, so that their foreheads were touching. He whispered something in Sicilian that sounded like a warning.

Rafael nodded.

Then, Carmine stalked off with his entourage of bodyguards, leaving his son, who looked wounded, watching him. He wandered toward Audrey, who said, "Are you okay? Is anyone out there hurt?"

He shook his head. "There was no sign of the men in town. They ran off before we could get to them."

"Who were they?"

"Nothing. We'll speak with those involved and get more details. It's nothing you should concern yourself with," he said, dazed, and then seemed to suddenly awaken. He took her arms. "I'm sorry, Audrey. Are you all right? I am sorry that this happened. We were having such a nice dinner, and now it is ruined."

Ruined seemed like an understatement. Rain ruined events. This felt catastrophic. Audrey was still shaking. The joyous mood from earlier had been shattered, and now everyone was somber. There was a dead body lying inside the tent.

"Bruno is dead," she murmured quietly.

Rafael's eyes shot to hers. "Who?"

"Bruno. Patty's boyfriend."

51

"Ah. I never met the man. Is everyone else—"

"No. There was one other man—"

"Luigi. My nephew."

That didn't help much. Everybody in this place was Rafael's nephew or cousin or niece or something. "Luigi has a minor wound in his shoulder. Nothing serious. I treated him. Seems like everyone else is all right." A sour feeling settled in her stomach as she caught sight of Patty, standing over the body of the boyfriend she'd been so excited for Audrey to meet. "Oh no."

"What is it?" Rafael said gently.

"I feel terrible. As a doctor, it's our job to assess the situation and tend to the most life-threatening emergencies first. And I didn't. If I had only gotten to Bruno first, he might still be alive."

Rafael smiled sadly. "You mustn't say things like that. You tended to Luigi as best you could and you did a wonderful job. We owe you a debt of gratitude again."

She shook her head and thought about the coin in her pocket. "No. Please."

"No, it's true. If not for you, we might have two deaths on our hands."

"It was just a flesh wound, really, and that's my job."

But Rafael refused to hear it, and continued to pour praise on her. She didn't really want to talk about it anymore, so she was happy when he changed the subject. "I am sure this is so awful for you. Would you like to return home? We can leave at once."

She nodded. All she wanted to do was put this awful night behind her. "Yes. I think that would be for the best."

"All right," he said, patting her hand. "Let me carry on with a few things, and then we'll head back to Mussomeli. I will bring you home, and return here so we can deal with what we need to deal with."

"You're not going to—"

He put a finger to his lips. "Audrey. It is not your concern."

"I'm just worried about you," she admitted. "As a friend, I mean."

He smiled. "All is fine, Audrey. I promise. Please, I should get to work right now. But if you pack your things, I'll meet you out front in, say, an hour?"

"Oh, of course, take your time," she said.

He went off to check on his other family members, and Audrey quickly escaped out of the tent. Outside, men were milling about, talking and decompressing. There was no sign of the terrible events that had just taken place.

She never wanted to go back there again. Ever. In fact, the whole place, which had once been beautiful and delightfully tacky, now took on a sinister air. She sucked in fresh air, trying to calm herself down.

Yes, it would be good to get away, as soon as possible.

When she headed back to the house to get her weekend bag, there were more people there, getting ready to leave. She floated around from group to group, listening in on the gossip. Some people seemed convinced it was one of the rival drug gangs from Palermo. Other people said that the getaway car belonged to one of Carmine's sworn enemies from his childhood. It seemed no one knew what to believe. There was a different story for every person there.

When Audrey grabbed her bag, she went out to the front of the mansion to wait for Rafael. As she stepped out, she saw an ambulance outside, lights flashing.

Paramedics were wheeling a gurney from the back of the house, down the sidewalk. There was a motionless, sheet-covered body atop it. Luigi was there, too. He climbed into the back of the ambulance. Patty followed close behind, shaking her head in disbelief. Stroking Pickle absently, she exchanged a few words with the paramedic, then turned and headed toward the front of the house. As she drew closer, Audrey could see the mascara streaked on her pink cheeks.

Poor girl, Audrey thought as the ambulance pulled away down the drive. *The gravity of the situation must be just setting in.*

She reached into her pocket and pulled out a tissue. She was about to hand it to the poor woman when Patty's face seemed to crumple and get even more wounded.

She ignored the tissue. "You're leaving? But you can't leave!" she whined.

"Well, I—"

"Bruno was going to stay with me. We were supposed to spend the weekend here together. And if he's gone . . . I can't spend the weekend alone in this house. I just can't." Her eyes were wide with fear.

"Oh, but you won't be alone. Carmine will be here, and there will be plenty of other guests staying, I'm su—"

"No! But I want you. You're a doctor. It's very reassuring to know that if I have any problems or anxiety, I can come to you."

"I'm a veterinarian."

"So?" She shuddered as she looked up at the house. "I need you. Knowing poor Bruno was killed here? I can't do it, Audrey. I can't."

She burst into tears. Audrey put an arm around her and directed her to sit on the top of the steps with her. "You and Bruno were together a long time, then."

She nodded. "Two months."

"Two . . ." Audrey frowned. "Months?"

"Yes." She finally took the tissue from Audrey and wiped at her eyes. "But we've known each other since we were ten years old."

"Wow. You must've been very close."

"He used to send me the cutest little texts, all the time. That's why I had a feeling something was wrong. I kept texting to see where he was, and he didn't respond."

"Where was he coming from? You said the university in Palermo?"

She nodded. "Luigi was picking him up, he said, and then they had a little errand to do for Carmine. He wouldn't tell me what it was. As women, we're not really supposed to get involved in their business."

Audrey wasn't sure she liked that idea, but she understood that was just how the mafia worked. "But you think it was something . . ." She stopped short of saying *illegal*. "For the . . . uh, family business?"

"I think? Maybe?" She shrugged.

Audrey watched as more people got into the cars and left. The C-shaped driveway was now nearly empty. Patty blew her nose loudly into the tissue.

"He was the love of my life. Really. We talked about marriage. A big wedding. My family's in Jersey but Bruno's from Sicily. We were going to fly them all out here. It was going to be a huge event. And now . . . " She closed her eyes and let out a long sigh. "I can't believe it. I can't believe he's gone."

Audrey touched her shoulder. "He's in a better place," she said, parroting what Patty had said to Aunt Angela earlier.

Patty stared in front of her, sniffling miserably. "You'll stay, right?"

Audrey looked down at her bag. "Uh . . . sure. I believe we were expected to. I was just thinking, that with everything that happened, it might be a good idea to . . . you know . . ."

Patty clapped her hands. "Oh my *gawd*." She grabbed Audrey's wrist tightly. "I just had the *best* idea."

Audrey wasn't sure she was ready to hear it. She'd probably be forced to go along with it, too, no matter what it was, because, well . . . mafia. "You did?"

She nodded, still gripping Audrey's wrist so hard, twisting it slightly so that the skin burned. "Yes. My room has a queen bed. You can *stay with me!*"

Audrey immediately bristled at the idea. "Oh, well . . . I'd have to check to see what plans Rafael . . ."

"You're not rooming with *him*, that's for sure."

Audrey stared at Patty, unsure of how to take that comment. She chalked it up to this being a traditional Catholic family. They probably didn't like any bedroom-sharing outside of marriage under the Piccolo family roof. That was fine with her. She didn't want to stay in a bedroom with Rafael. But she didn't want to room with Patty, either. She'd been praying she'd get her *own* room.

The door behind them opened, and Rafael stepped out, carrying his own bag. "Did Luigi go to the hospital?"

"There he is!" Patty shouted, more back to her old self as she jumped up and grabbed ahold of his wrist. "Look, I was just trying to convince Audrey to stay. I need her."

He frowned. "I don't know . . . With everything that happened, Audrey's clearly upset. I should get her—"

"Come on. Carmine's going to need someone to pick Luigi up from the hospital tonight. They're doping him up on painkillers but you know he's not going to want to stay there overnight."

Rafael considered this, nodded, and looked at Audrey. "Are you okay with that?"

She nodded. At this point, she didn't think she had much of a choice.

Patty squealed and grabbed Audrey's arm. "I told her she could stay in a room with me!"

Audrey expected Rafael to argue and say that there were other plans, but she was surprised at how quickly he agreed. "Sounds like you have it all figured out."

Patty let out a sigh of relief as she went inside. "I am so glad youse guys are staying! It really takes a load off my mind. This old house is like the Haunted Mansion sometimes. Gives me the creeps, with all those freakish statues staring down at you. *Gawd.* The other night I nearly had a heart attack."

When they were alone, Rafael leaned over and grabbed Audrey's bag, smiling at her. "I'm glad we decided to stay. It will mean a lot to Patty. So thank you."

"It's no problem at all," she assured him.

He stared at her for what felt like a beat too long, and for a moment, she thought he might try to lean in and kiss her. But he hadn't even been thinking about sharing a room with her. That seemed to be the last thing on his mind. So maybe this wasn't a date?

As if to confirm the fact, he dropped his gaze. "What do you say we all go inside and get some of my dad's pasta? I'm starving."

"Sounds good," she said, following him inside.

CHAPTER TEN

So that was how, at nine o'clock at night, a number of the Piccolo family wound up sitting around that massive center island in the kitchen, eating Carmine's famous pasta.

Carmine wasn't there—apparently, he had business to attend to, *revenge* business—but there were several cousins and aunts and uncles there, eating bowls of linguini.

Rafael grinned at Audrey as she shoveled the stuff into her mouth. She couldn't get it in fast enough. "You like, hmm?"

She swallowed. "It's so good. I've never had anything like it before."

"I know," he said, reaching over and grabbing the oregano. "If he was on one of those cooking shows, he'd win the whole thing."

"Do you cook like this, too?" she asked him. "Because I wouldn't mind some pasta in addition to those oranges."

Rafael shook his head. "No. Unfortunately, that's one family secret that he will take to the grave."

Patty nodded. "Right! He doesn't tell anyone what he puts in his pasta sauce. He makes everyone leave the kitchen when he makes it. It's always been a secret."

"That's crazy. You'd think he'd want *someone* to know it, so that he could pass it down."

"I have a feeling that one day, when Uncle Carmine's gone, Rafe will get a key to a lockbox somewhere, and go in, expecting jewels and other riches . . . and instead find a recipe card," Patty said, pointing her fork at her cousin. "You watch."

Franco, sitting across from Audrey, nodded. "You can go into the restaurant business, if nothing else, cousin. Or maybe you can sell his sauce."

Rafael expertly twirled the linguini on his fork. "Or maybe I'll just work to keep it a secret from you rascals."

Audrey cleaned her plate easily, got another helping, and slurped that up, too. She got to the point that even though she was full, she still didn't want to stop eating. She wished she had a bigger stomach so she could enjoy it longer.

But then she felt her stomach pressing against her waistband, and decided it was probably not a good idea to get thirds.

She sipped her red wine from the Piccolo family vineyard, and looked around at her companions. They were all talking loudly, arguing, joking, enjoying a regular family meal . . . despite the horrors they'd witnessed only hours ago.

She yawned.

Patty picked up on it right away. "Come with me. I'll show you our room, roomie!"

"Goodnight," Rafael said, standing and nodding to her as she slid off her chair. "I'm going to the hospital to check on Luigi anyway. I will see you tomorrow."

"Will you be . . . okay?" she asked. After all, Luigi and Bruno hadn't been so lucky.

He smiled. "Yes. We'll be fine."

She said her goodnights to him and the other people around the table, then let Patty guide her up the long, sweeping staircase to the second floor. There, she opened double doors to a large suite. Audrey looked around, awed.

"I know, right? I had a roomie where I live in *Nork*. But our whole place back there would probably fit in the bathroom here!" she said with a laugh. "So you can see why I'm not in a rush to get back. Plus, I'm between jobs now."

"What do you do?"

"Nail technician," she said, wiggling her fingers, looking at Audrey's. "You could use a manicure."

Audrey fisted her hands. "Oh. It's hard, since I work with my hands a lot, you know. And there isn't a place in Mussomeli. So I mostly just—"

"I'll give you one!" she offered excitedly, grabbing for Audrey's hand.

Audrey could just imagine the two of them, sitting on the giant queen bed, trading stories and painting each other's nails, like at a regular preteen slumber party. She yawned again.

"Sure, but do you mind if we do it tomorrow? I'm a little tired."

"Of course. I'll let you have the bathroom first," Patty said, flopping on a chair. "This is going to be so much fun, *roomie!*"

*

58

As tired as Audrey had been, when she finally reclined in the bed, she wound up staring at the ceiling. As upset as Patty had been about the death of Bruno, she soon drifted off to sleep, her breathing becoming slow and even.

Audrey turned on her side, trying to push the worries of the day out of her mind. The more she did, the more she worried. She thought about that poor Bruno, dying, sputtering his last word, *Fiori*.

What did that mean? Did he really just want to make sure there were flowers at his funeral?

And was it really a rival gang that had done it? Was Carmine's group planning revenge as she lay there? Maybe she would wake up tomorrow and find herself in the midst of an all-out war.

Then she wondered about Rafael. He'd brought her all the way here to meet his family, and yes, part of it was at the request of his grandfather, Don Piccolo. But was part of it because he liked her? Sometimes she felt like he was flirting, but sometimes she thought he was just being nice. It was all so confusing.

Her thoughts wandered to Nick. It was a chillier evening than usual, and Nick always loved to come in when it was cooler, and snuggle on her bed. What if he was outside, wanting to come in and get warm?

It was that thought that made her pick up her phone and check the time. Just after midnight. Though it was cozy under the covers, she couldn't bear the thought of being nice and warm while Nick was outside, freezing.

Pulling back the comforter, she slid out, being careful not to wake Patty. She went to the door and pulled it open, surprised to see bright light in the hallway. Pausing to let her eyes adjust to the brightness, she poked her head out and peered up and down the long hallway, decorated in old tapestries.

There was no one there, but she could hear voices coming from somewhere downstairs. One of them sounded like Rafael.

As she crept downstairs, she made a promise to herself that she wouldn't eavesdrop. *You know what they do to eavesdroppers? Murder. Maybe worse. Dismemberment.*

So the plan was to simply go downstairs, slip through the front door, look around for Nick to make sure he was okay, and then bring him back upstairs. That was it.

And it almost worked that way.

The second she opened the door, she saw Nick curled up on the welcome mat. He looked miserable, his little body shivering.

She crouched in front of him. "Hey, Bub. So you don't like sleeping outside, huh? What did you ever do before me?"

Elated, he jumped into her arms. She brought him inside and closed the front door, stroking his fur. Pickle was on his bed in the kitchen, and everyone in the house had fawned over him. *I'm sure no one will mind if I bring my pet upstairs.*

She'd crossed the black-and-white checkerboard floor of the foyer and was just about to climb the steps when she heard Rafael say, in a voice that sounded a bit strained, "I still think that's dangerous, Padre."

Audrey stopped, listening. Carmine said, "It doesn't matter. Luigi. Continue."

Luigi? The man who was shot? Audrey couldn't help herself. She wanted to know more about what had happened. She found her feet dragging her in the direction of the office where she'd first me Rafael's powerful father.

Why were they speaking English? The reason only occurred to her when she reached the doorway and saw the shadows of all the men. Perhaps some of the American relations didn't speak Sicilian. But all of them seemed to go still as Luigi began his story.

Of course they did. It was a story all of them had been waiting to hear. Audrey found herself holding her breath in anticipation.

Well, if they didn't want me listening in, they shouldn't be speaking English, she thought, pressing up against the wall and listening as she petted Nick, who was already falling asleep in her arms.

"Like I said," Luigi went on, his voice faint, likely from the painkillers, "I went to the university to pick up Bruno because Patty told me his car was in the shop. I got him, no problem, and we stopped at the gas station in town to fill up the tank."

The gas station, Audrey thought. *I wonder if it was the same one we went to.*

"We were just getting back into the car when someone opened fire. Bruno was shot, then I was. I noticed Bruno was bleeding real bad so I brought him here."

Rafael said, "Yes, but how do you know it's them?"

"Who else could it be?" Carmine growled. "They have been a thorn in our sides for far too long. This needs to end now."

Luigi said, "I know it was them. I saw Marco a few minutes before, when we drove into town. He must've seen me, and decided to make good on his promise from last month. To end me."

Rafael's voice was calm, in control. "To end you? Because of the—
"

"Because I let Vito Capaldi take the rap for that last deal, outside of Palermo. The one I told you about. The sentence was handed down last week. He got two years."

Capaldi, Audrey thought, hugging Nick tightly to her chest. *Why does that name sound familiar?*

Audrey peered through a narrow gap in the open doorway to see Rafael, still in his suit, though the tie was open and several buttons of his shirt were undone. He had more than a little five o'clock shadow, which he rubbed as he hunched over his father's desk, deep in thought. "Yes. I will agree this doesn't look good. But I don't think we should rush into war."

"Rush. *Rush?*" Carmine's laugh was bitter. "This has been going on as long as you've been alive, boy. And you don't want to rush? *Dio.* We have been patient long enough. That time is passed. Now, we need to take action, before they move to wipe us off the map once and for all."

Rafael shook his head. "I don't know—"

"This is an act of war, and if you don't see it, son, you'll never make a good don," the man said, looking from Rafael to Alessandro. "Your grandfather had six of us to choose from, to continue the Piccolo dynasty. He chose me, not my older brother, and why? Because I had the foresight to recognize what our family needed, and the courage to do what needed to be done."

Alessandro rolled his eyes. He was busy fiddling with what looked like a Rubik's Cube. "Yeah, Dad, you tell us that like, every day."

Carmine thrust a finger at them. "Because you two *sciocchi* need to learn it."

Rafael hung his head. "I know, but—"

"Sometimes I don't know if you do know that." He motioned him away and studied the rest of the men. "This is what we're going to do. Tomorrow morning, you show up at Marco Capaldi's place, and send whoever's there a strong message. You understand?"

They all nodded, as something tickled at the back of Audrey's mind.

Marco Capaldi.

Marco Capaldi.

Marco . . . where had she heard that name before?

61

Suddenly, she found herself standing outside the antiques shop with the old owner, Flavio, negotiating the price of the beautiful mirror. The man who had helped her had been so nice, and when he'd introduced himself to her . . .

Oh no.

And now these men were going to *send him a message.* And not with paper. With bullets, and blood, and . . .

Audrey hadn't meant to do it, but she suddenly let out a gasp so loud, every face in the office turned to look at her.

CHAPTER ELEVEN

Before Audrey's heart could even jump into her throat, the men broke into action. They were clearly used to acting on a moment's notice, because they all advanced on her.

She took a step back, and Nick must've heard the commotion, because he woke, his ears perking up and the hair on the top of his head standing straight up in warning position. He leapt into attack mode, hissing at them.

"Shh," she whispered to him, petting him into submission, then plastered a fake smile on her face. In her head, she chanted, *I have the Piccolo coin. I have the Piccolo coin. I am the Favored One. They love me. I think.* "Hi!"

Rafael held his arms out to his sides, holding the rest of them back. "Audrey," he said, kindly but cautiously. "What are you doing up?"

"Oh. Uh, I forgot about Nick," she said, holding him up for their inspection. "So I came down to get him, and I heard Luigi's voice. I just wanted to make sure he was okay."

"I'm okay," Luigi muttered.

"What did you *hear*, exactly?" Alessandro said, eyes narrowed.

Oh no, Audrey thought, now swallowing in vain to release the heart that had so tightly jammed itself in her esophagus. *This is the part where they take out their guns and I sleep with the fishes.*

"Nothing much . . . just some things . . ."

They all stared at her, disbelieving. Suddenly, the Piccolo coin didn't seem nearly so special.

These men were clearly professionals. They made people crack under pressure for a living. She could already feel it happening. A bead of sweat trickled down her ribcage. "I heard you mention something about a Marco Capaldi."

The name seemed to inject tension into the room, because the men stiffened. One of the men, by the fireplace, threw up his hands and let out what had to be an Italian curse. Rafael held up his hands and said, plaintively, "Audrey, Audrey wait. Whatever you heard—"

"Well, you see, I don't think you have the right man, because I met Marco Capaldi. And he was a very nice man."

Their eyes seemed to narrow in unison.

That's true, Audrey. There are plenty of "very nice men" who are actually serial killers.

"Where did you meet him, Audrey?" Rafael asked.

"Oh. At the gas station. Remember? When I left you and went into that antiques store? He was there."

Carmine swung around to look at Rafael. "You knew Capaldi was in the area, and you didn't say anything?"

He shook his head. "I didn't know. I didn't see him. And Audrey certainly had no idea who he was—"

"That's right," Audrey said. "He wasn't wearing a sign that said, *I'm Mafia*. And he certainly didn't seem like the type who'd go around offing people in the middle of the street. He was kind. He helped me with a mirror."

Carmine frowned. "A mirror?"

She nodded. "*Lo specchio*. I can show it to you, if you . . ."

She trailed off when he waved her off with a grunt and stalked back to his desk. He clearly didn't care. He slipped into his chair and scrubbed his hands down his face. "Just . . . Rafi. Sandro. Franco. Take care of it. Tomorrow."

She looked at Rafael, who was gritting his teeth, clearly disappointed with the decision. And he had every right to be! He'd just been ordered to kill, as if it was nothing.

"But wait!" she blurted, before she had a chance to think about what she was doing.

Carmine stared at her, his expression saying his thoughts very clearly: *How dare you? No one does that to me.*

She thought about her Piccolo coin. That, at least, should've given her some special standing, right? She'd been of assistance to them in Mussomeli, and then to Pickle, and later, Luigi. She'd earned the right to speak without getting herself offed. At least, she hoped she had.

So she said, very carefully, "I understand your families have been at odds for years, and this has always been brewing. But all I'm saying is that you don't know for sure if Marco is responsible, do you?"

He made like he was waving her off again, so she spoke quickly.

"I mean, yes, he was in the area. Yes, you're right, it's a remarkable coincidence. But you don't have any proof, do you, that it was him. Do you?"

Carmine thought for a moment. Then he said, "Luigi, did you actually see the guy?"

64

Luigi straightened. "Well, no, but—"

"Then before you just go out putting hits on people willy-nilly, shouldn't you be sure? Especially since you know they're going to retaliate." Her voice, a squeak to begin with, cracked. She shrugged. "I mean, you don't want to bring all this pain to your family on a hunch, do you?"

They looked at her like she was speaking Russian.

Rafael said, "So what you're saying is, you want us to be sure first. How?"

She shrugged. "Gather evidence. Build the case. You know. Investigate. Make sure."

"You mean, like cops have to do?" Alessandro asked, as if it was so foreign to him, he couldn't wrap his head around it.

"Well . . .yeah. Maybe. Like that."

Carmine's stare was so hard, she almost had to look away. Her face burned hot under it. But he broke it first and looked down at his desk.

She continued, trying to seal the deal with some honey. "It's a known fact that ninety-eight percent of turf wars begin as a result of a misunderstanding. I like your family. And I'd hate for your people to be a part of that statistic."

He let out a long breath of air and then looked at the men. "All right. Fine. We'll get our proof first, and then we'll strike."

Audrey let out the breath she was holding in relief. She'd prevented a war, but for how long? "Great."

She was about to retreat, Nick in her arms, when she heard his voice say, "Where will you look into first, in order to get this proof of yours?"

She looked up, surprised to find him staring at *her*.

"Oh. No. I'm sorry. There's some misunderstanding. Actually, I just said you should find proof. I didn't offer that I was going to help find it." She hooked a thumb behind her, pointing in the direction of what she thought was Mussomeli, babbling. "I'm not skilled in that. I'm a vet, remember? I have my practice, and I need to go back to—"

"Rafael told all of us what you did, back in Mussomeli. How you investigated that murder and confirmed who the killer was. We know you have some experience with this," he said, leaning forward, smiling. "Yes?"

"Yes, a little. But I'm sure one of your other men knows the family, knows the area, better than I do, which is important in order to—"

"But my men are biased. They fly off the handle. They go and investigate the Capaldis, see something they don't like, I can't stop them from taking out their vengeance right there." He nodded definitively, and Audrey knew there was no changing his mind. "But you . . . you are impartial, yes? And that is what we need."

This was bad. She had to get back to Mussomeli. Concetta was good, but she couldn't expect the girl to handle everything for any longer than the weekend. Not to mention that this business was dangerous. Men had been shot.

"I'd really love to, but—"

"Then you will help us. That is settled."

Not *Can you help us?* or *Please help us.* No, he'd clearly said, *You will help us.*

Yep, that was an offer she couldn't refuse.

"All right," she said. "But I do have to get back to my practice. So—"

"That is fine. I will give you until Sunday night . . . say, seven on Sunday night . . . to see what you can find. If you find nothing, then Monday morning, we'll proceed with our plan to pay a little visit to Marco Capaldi. Yes?"

She swallowed. Sunday night. "But it's Sunday . . . morning." Barely.

"You have a problem with that?"

The only appropriate answer was to shake her head. She backed away and started to head to the staircase, as Carmine called after her, "What is that . . . animal?"

"Oh. It's a fox." She showed it to him.

He stared at it. "First that ugly dog. Now this? I don't like animals in my house."

Rafael cleared his throat. "I told her she could bring it. She'll keep it in her room. You won't even know it's here."

Grunting, he waved them away.

Rafael wrapped an arm around her neck and took her out to the foyer. At the foot of the stairs, he turned to her and said, "I am so sorry."

She groaned. She wanted to kick herself. "Oh, no. It's not your fault. I guess I stepped in this one myself. Me and my big mouth."

"Don't feel bad. I appreciate you trying to buy time."

"What do you mean?"

He checked over his shoulder, then looked toward the office and pulled her aside, into an alcove.

"Unfortunately, you can poke around all you want. My father is right. This has been brewing for too long, and perhaps I've been blind to it, in wanting to keep things quiet. You won't be able to find anything. Marco Capaldi is the killer, and that's all there is to it."

She stared up at him. "You want to go to war?"

"No. Of course not." He closed his eyes, and she could tell the idea distressed him greatly. "But some things are inevitable. At this point, I don't think there's any way of avoiding it. Not now. I've done all I can."

"Why is your father war-happy?"

"He's not. He's simply dealt with too many of these instances, and he's tired of it. This is the last straw." He rubbed his eyes tiredly. "I just wish there was something else I can do. I've convinced him to keep a peace, however precarious, for the sake of our family. But it looks as though those days are over."

"I don't believe that," she said, though now, she was having her doubts. "If he didn't see Marco, there's always a chance."

He gave her a sad smile. "You know, a lot of these family businesses like ours have settled down, playing by the rules, in recent years. We have been. But we can't ignore this. If we do, it'll bring great shame upon our family. We have to answer."

Her heart went out to him. He wasn't like his father, or the other men in this family. He wanted peace. Now, she understood why he'd moved out to Mussomeli. He'd wanted to escape this kind of life. "I'm sorry, too."

He studied her closely. "Are you sure you'll be okay?"

"Yes. I'm just going to go to sleep."

"All right. Good night. *Again.*" He gave her a small smile.

She smiled back. For a moment, she thought he might lean in and kiss her, but then he simply ruffled Nick's fur and turned away from her.

She yawned and climbed the steps to her bedroom, feeling terrible. If only she hadn't gotten out of bed! Maybe then, she wouldn't have gotten herself into this mess.

In the bedroom, it was warm and comfortable. Patty was fast asleep. Audrey placed Nick on the pillow beside her and climbed into bed, trying not to make a noise. Her mind swam with thoughts and ideas for the next day, none of which she was that excited to pursue. *I guess I'll have to go into town tomorrow. Interview people. See if there were any witnesses to the shooting. Maybe find Capaldi, and see if he has an alibi.*

Barely more than sixteen hours of time to prevent a war. Would it be enough?

CHAPTER TWELVE

The following morning, Audrey was awakened by a scream.

She sat bolt upright in bed and wiped her eyes, just in time to see Patty streaking across the bedroom, golf club in hand, swinging it around wildly.

"Wild animal!" she screeched.

"Wild animal?" Audrey asked in wonder, throwing the comforter off her body and jumping up. "Where?"

"It must've gotten in through the open window! It was on our bed! I thought it was going to eat our faces!" she shouted, swinging again as a flash of red dove under the bed.

Suddenly, Audrey woke up just enough to understand what was going on. "Wait!" she said, lunging at Patty as she dropped to her hands and knees to root around under the bed. She grabbed the top of the putter and held it. "That's not a wild animal. That's Nick!"

"Who?"

"My pet fox."

"Pet?" Patty rolled over and fell on her backside, then blew a puff of curly hair out of her face, still breathing hard. "Oh. Really?"

"Yeah. Sorry. I forgot to tell you. He was too cold last night outside, so I brought him in. You were asleep."

She pushed aside the sheets and peered into the darkness. Nick was sitting in the center there, licking his paws. He didn't seem to be too traumatized by his run-in with Patty's golf club. She motioned him out, and he jumped into Audrey's arms.

"Oh. He's kind of cute," she said, grabbing a little pink satin robe and pulling it over her slim frame. "I'm going down to breakfast. You coming with?"

Audrey shook her head. "I have to get into town early. I'll get something there," she said, wondering if she could walk it. The town hadn't been very far away, from what she remembered.

"What are you up to?" she asked, grinning slyly. "Anything fun?"

Audrey wasn't sure what she was allowed to say and what she wasn't, so she just smiled. "No. Not really. Just errands."

"Okay, well. You have to try the *limoncello* jam when you have a chance. It's made with lemons from the grove here. It's to die for! And it has a lot of grappa in it." She bumped the door open with her hip and sauntered out.

For a moment, Audrey had to wonder if she even remembered her poor Bruno. She looked down at Nick. "Bub, I've got a lot to do today."

As if understanding, he jumped from her arms and dashed to the windowsill. He climbed onto it and slipped out the window, which had been open a crack.

"Nick!"

She ran to it and realized there was an eave directly underneath her. The last thing she saw was Nick disappearing behind a corner of the house. Off again on his adventures.

"Have fun," she murmured. "I know I won't."

Then she rushed into the bathroom to get ready for the day.

As she showered, she replayed the events of the previous night in her head. She had to admit, it made perfect sense that Carmine would want her to investigate the shooting. After all, the other men were hot-headed. Rafael was the calmest of all of them, and yet even he had much invested in his own family. She really was the only one who could look into it without jumping to conclusions.

And even though she wasn't family, she felt that strong sense of justice nagging at her. It was always the same. As much as she wanted to stay out of danger, another, bigger part of her usually popped up, wanting the criminals to pay for what they'd done. Poor Bruno. And if he hadn't done it, poor Marco.

Poor *everyone*, if she didn't succeed.

As she changed into a short-sleeve chambray dress with a tie on the side, she checked her phone. Only ten hours to get some answers.

Thanks for the ticking clock, Carmine. She felt it hanging on her, like a noose around her neck.

She slipped into her espadrilles and headed down the stairs. As she did, she found Alessandro, wearing a tech shirt with sweat stains on the chest, and running shorts.

"*Ciao.* If it isn't the lovely *dottore*," he said with a grin. "You are off to find some answers, eh?"

She nodded, a little disconcerted by the way he was staring at her. If he was fourteen years Rafael's junior, that meant that he was in his twenties, so quite a bit younger than she was. And she was here as

Rafael's date. So why was he looking at her like he wanted to take a bite of her? He was handsome, yes, but there was something brash, cocky, a little *off* about him.

"Maybe. I was looking for your brother."

He didn't answer her right away. Instead, he reached down, grabbed the hem of his shirt, and pulled it up over his head, revealing a set of abs that made her think of Mason. Grinning wickedly, he wiped his forehead with it and said, "Why are you wasting time with him?"

She averted her eyes and tucked a strand of hair behind her ear. "I just wanted to borrow his car."

"Detective Audrey has places to go, eh?" He strutted through the foyer, tossing his sweaty shirt over his shoulder, and motioned her to follow him with a hooked finger. "Probably in the kitchen."

When they got to the kitchen, though, it was empty, except for Pickle, who bounded up to her, his toenails clacking on the travertine tile floors. Scooping him up and petting him, she looked around. She expected, at least, to find Patty there, eating breakfast. But though there was a pot of limoncello jam sitting on the island, there was no one in sight.

Alessandro opened the fridge and pulled out a bottle of water. He threw his head back and chugged it, taking his time savoring it, and then looked back at her. For a moment, he almost seemed surprised to see her still standing there.

Then he said, "Nice day out. I was thinking about going for a swim later. Want to go with me?"

"As appetizing as that sounds, I think . . . no. Well, it was nice talking to you. But it looks like Rafael's gone, and I'd better be on my—"

"Oh, right," he said, snapping his fingers. "I forgot. Rafael had to leave early on business with my dad. They cancelled all the events for this weekend because they had a lot of things to do."

Her heart slumped. It was going to make finding answers very difficult if she didn't have a mode of transportation. And business? Was it dangerous? "Business? Where?"

"Palermo, I think. He's always taking him places. Teaching him the ropes. Leaving me to live my life of leisure. Which I intend to do to the fullest." He leaned toward her, elbows on the counter. "Come on, Audrey. I'm a hot mafia bad boy. Don't tell me you're not the least bit interested in me, because I will not believe it."

71

She shook her head. "All right. I won't tell you that. Even though it's true."

He gave her a wounded look. "Come on. Where looks are concerned, I blow my brother away. If you're waiting for him to make a move, you're gonna be waiting a long time. So you might as well have some fun with me. Trust me. I *am* fun."

"I'm sure you are, but I'm not waiting on him," she insisted, really wanting to get away from this conversation. "Alessandro. Rafael and I are just friends. That's all."

He nodded slowly, like he didn't believe her. Then he shrugged and reached into his pocket and pulled out a set of keys, which he pushed across the center island to her. "He told you to help yourself to his car."

She rolled her eyes and scooped up the keys. *You could've told me that about twenty minutes ago.* Checking her phone, she winced. It was eight a.m. *Only eleven hours left.* "Thanks. I'll see you. If Rafael comes home and he's looking for me—"

"Whatever. I'm going in the pool," he muttered, jogging off. He opened the back door and slipped outside without another look in her direction.

She turned to leave, but not before watching him peel off his sneakers and gym shorts, then dive, in the tiniest of Speedos, into the pool. *Oh boy,* she thought, shaking her head.

Hurrying to the front of the house, she opened the door and saw Rafael's black convertible among all the other black sedans parked in the driveway. *Goodness, is it a requirement that they all have black cars?* she wondered as she made her way there.

The second she put her hand on the driver's side door handle, the front door of the mansion clicked open behind her. "Wait up!" a voice called. "*Awwww*-drey! *Awd!* Wait!"

Audrey turned to find Patty jogging toward her as fast as her tiny kitten heels could carry her. She was wearing tight, zebra-print leggings and a flowered, off-the-shoulder blouse, her piles of wild hair somehow sprayed into submission, an undefinable style that would've taken up its own zip code in the States. "Oh. Hi. Did I forget something?"

"No. Hey," she said, popping her gum, then taking a long string of it from her mouth. "So like, I heard you were going out. And I was thinking, like, yeah. I want to go do this, too. It'll be fun. We can be like, you know. Thelma and Louise. Or like, Cagney and Lacey."

Audrey had spent enough time in this world to feel more like she was in an episode of *The Sopranos.* "What are we doing again?"

72

"You know! Luigi told me all about it. How you volunteered to confirm who Bruno's killer is. Tell me, how did that come about?"

Patty stared her expectantly. Audrey opened her mouth to speak, but Patty slapped her on the arm.

"Doesn't matter. It was really amazing that you did that. And I thought, wow. That's so brave. I always feel like our guys are rushing into stupid situations they can't control. It made total sense to me."

"You think?"

She nodded. "Oh my gosh. Our guys, always shooting first, asking questions later. Dumb, dumb, dumb. So I want to do it, too. I must. For Bruno."

"You mean . . ."

"I want to be with you. I want to ask questions, too. Get it?"

Audrey hesitated. She actually wouldn't mind having the company. Patty probably knew the area way better that her GPS did. But Carmine had put Audrey on this mission because she was impartial. How impartial would the victim's girlfriend be? It seemed like it was defeating the purpose. "Well, I—"

"I mean, where would you even start, otherwise?"

"I was going to start at the gas station, ask questions, and—"

She stopped mid-sentence. As logical a starting place as that was, she remembered the difficulty she'd had securing the mirror. And that was simple. *Lo specchio.* What did she actually think she'd accomplish interviewing locals, with such a big language barrier in the way?

She probably needed the help of someone more local than she was. And since Patty had been coming here all her life, she probably knew a bit more than she did. "Do you happen to speak Sicilian?"

Patty shrugged. "Sure. A little."

Audrey sighed. After being propositioned by Alessandro, she didn't really have the energy left to argue anymore. So she flipped the locks and motioned to the passenger's side. "All right, then. Get in. Let's go."

CHAPTER THIRTEEN

It took Audrey a little while to get the hang of driving Rafael's car, but once she did, it was actually an enjoyable ride to town. The weather was sunny and warm, without a cloud in the sky, and the air smelled sweetly of the lemons in the grove at the front of Cielo d'Azzurro. With the top of the convertible down, it almost felt like a pleasant Sunday drive.

Except for that ticking clock.

As they drove, Patty did most of the talking, chatting on about her life in Newark, New Jersey. She'd lived her whole life there, went to cosmetology school, and had started working as a technician in a place on Route One when a few years later, she felt like she was missing out. She met Bruno at a family gathering in Palermo that they went to every year, fell in love, and they'd been together ever since.

"You know it is love when the place you always felt was your home doesn't feel like your home anymore," she said, twirling a lock of hair around her finger as she gazed at the rolling countryside.

"Really?" Audrey asked.

"Yep. I thought I'd miss the States so much, but I never did. Not with Bruno around. I knew he was my home."

Audrey didn't know what to say. She wasn't sure there was anything she could tell her that would make her feel better about Bruno's death, so she said, "I've been in Sicily five months, and sometimes, I'm still not sure I belong here."

"Do you have a boyfriend?"

Audrey glanced at her. That was a rather odd question, considering that Rafael had brought her to this place for the weekend. "No one serious, honestly. Rafael's been nice, and I've met a lot of people I'd call friends. But I just don't know. Sometimes I miss my family back in America so much, and all I want to do is go back. But then something happens, and I'm so happy I'm here. It's like a roller coaster."

"You'll figure it out," Patty said. Now she was twirling her gum around her finger. "It takes as long as it takes, you know?"

"Yeah. I guess."

"By the way, Sandro really seems to like you."

She cringed. "Sandro? Well, he's—"

"Yeah. He likes everything female. He usually brings home girls who look like they should be on a street corner somewhere. He comes on to me, too, at least once, at every family gathering, and I'm his cousin! But it'd be nice to finally see him settle down with a girl who is actually . . . normal."

Audrey laughed. "Well, I'm here with Rafael, so . . ."

"I don't think Rafael would mind. He likes you a lot, too."

Okay, that was strange. Were they such a tight-knit family that they didn't mind sharing women?

She still hadn't thought of a reply to that remark when they pulled up into a parking space near the curb of the gas station. As they arrived there, they noticed police cars gathered at one corner. A couple of officers were together, speaking.

When Audrey stepped out of the car, she noticed Patty's eyes were fastened on the spot. She'd gone pale.

"Come on," she said to the girl, nudging her toward the antiques store. "Let's go into this store. I'll show you where I first met Marco Capaldi."

Her head swung toward Audrey. "Wait. You met him?"

She nodded.

"I've never even laid eyes on him. What did he say to you? Was he as big and mean as they say?"

"Nope. He was a gentleman. He couldn't have been nicer."

"That's crazy. Of course, he didn't have a reason to hate you. If he knew you were Rafe's guest for this weekend, I doubt he would've been so nice."

"True. But it's hard to believe that he—that any of the people I ate dinner with last night, really—could be cold-blooded killers."

She nodded. "I know. Sometimes I think they act so childish. It really is a shame. But at least it's not the way it was ages ago. They're really getting away from the crime. Or at least, they're getting smarter about it, so it's not nearly as violent as it once was." She shrugged. "That's what Bruno told me."

"How did Bruno get involved in it?" Audrey asked.

"The way most young guys do. He was friends with Luigi all through school. And then he just got accepted into the fold as one of their brothers. That's how I met Bruno. Luigi has always been one of my closest family members. We kind of grew up together, through the years, seeing each other at family reunions. Luigi introduced us."

"I didn't know that people who aren't part of the family could be a part of it."

"Oh, sure. I mean, he'd never get promoted as fast as, say, Alessandro, but he was very loyal."

They crossed the street to the antiques shop. The porch was just as littered as the day before, except for the open spot where the mirror once stood. Patty made a face. "Gross. This stuff is such junk."

"You don't like antiques?"

"No. Ew. They're so weird. Nothing in my place in *Nork* was more than five years old. I get tired of something . . ." She mimed tossing something away.

"Well, I guess you don't have to worry about overspending here," Audrey said as she opened the door. Again, the little bell above the door jingled, and they were faced with piles and piles of assorted knickknacks.

She turned toward Patty, who was making a face, her eyes volleying around the place as if they didn't know where to settle first.

"I forgot. The owner, Flavio, doesn't speak any English at all. So do you think you can translate if I ask him some questions?"

Patty shrugged. "Maybe. I'm a little rusty. My mother's much better than I am."

There was a slight shuffling coming from the back of the store, and then the old, stooped man appeared, tilting his head back to inspect them through his bifocals. "Eh?"

"*Ciao, Flavio?*" She started, stumbling a bit as she added, "*Ti ricordi di me, da ieri?*"

She was simply asking him if he remembered her from yesterday, but he was already staring at her like she had three heads.

"Um, *lo specchio?*"

His eyes narrowed. Then they filled with recognition, and he nodded. "Ah, *si. Lo specchio. Si.*"

Good. Progress had been made.

Then she realized that she had no idea how to say the rest of what she wanted to say. "Patty, I think this is where I'm going to need your help. Could ask him if I could ask him a couple questions about the man who came in yesterday and helped translate for me? Tall, well-built, dark hair, dark eyes. Maybe about forty-five years old?"

She nodded. Then she spoke, with all the accent and inflection of a native Sicilian, to him. She might have thought she was rusty, but she didn't sound that way to Audrey. She sounded wonderful. Audrey stared at her in wonder.

And clearly, Flavio understood, because he nodded and said, even before she was done, *"Si. Marco. Si."*

"Oh, so you *do* know him?" Audrey asked, excited now.

Patty translated, and when the man spoke, she nodded. "He says that Marco is a very good customer. Comes in here all the time." She shrugged. "Guess *he's* a fan of all this junk."

"Does he know where he lives?"

Patty asked, and in a moment, came with an answer. "He says that Marco Capaldi always buys furniture for his place here. He lives in the big villa on the north side of town, overlooking the city. The one with the blue shutters. I know the one. You can't miss it." She snorted. "I always thought it was a nice house, but it must be *super* ugly inside if he gets all his furniture here."

"We should go there and ask him questions," Audrey mused, but then a dose of reality seeped in. "Wait, can you? Do you think he knows who you are?"

"Doubtful. If I've never seen him, he's probably never seen me either. Besides, he's dumb as a stump."

"How do you know?"

"He's a Capaldi, so I bet you he is. I think we can fool him."

Audrey wasn't so sure. She needed answers, and now. Checking her phone—the time was steadily ticking away—she motioned to Flavio. "Can you ask him what he knows about the shooting that happened nearby?"

She translated. Flavio nodded and spoke. Patty said, "He was in the store when he heard the gunshots. But by the time he came out of the store, it was already over and two men got into a Mercedes and drove away. That was Bruno and Luigi. He went over to the corner, but there was nothing but a bit of blood. So he really didn't see anything."

"So it happened on that corner across the street, where the police were parked?"

Patty nodded. That was only half a block away, practically right outside the front door, but it made sense that Flavio hadn't seen much. The windows of the old store were cloudy, and mostly concealed by piles of junk, and Flavio was an old man.

"We should go over there and check it out," she said, backing away. *"Grazie, Flavio."*

He nodded and went off, grabbing a broom to sweep the floors, and Audrey retreated to the street. On the porch, she stood there, checking out the surroundings. This small area on the edge of town was probably the most bustling corner in this sleepy little enclave. Surrounded by rocky cliffs, it seemed away from the rest of the world, a bit like Mussomeli. As the first intersection one ran into while traveling in from the east, this corner probably saw a fair number of transients, stopping to get gas before heading on the rest of their journey.

Maybe a transient had committed the shootings? If so, how would she ever find evidence of that to convince Carmine not to attack?

If she couldn't find out who killed Bruno, maybe the best she could do was find an alibi for Capaldi.

"I know that look. What's going through your head, girl?" Patty said.

Audrey shrugged. "Well, I was just thinking. This is Marco Capaldi's neighborhood. He visits this store often. Doesn't it seem unlikely to you that he'd commit murder in his own backyard?"

She inspected her fingernails. "I don't know. I don't really put anything past the Capaldis. Or our guys, either, for that matter. Sometimes I think they're so blinded by their hate for each other that they'll do anything." She sighed, but then her eyes fastened on something. "Oh! Look at this!"

At first, Audrey couldn't be sure what she was referring to, among all the junk. But then, as Patty cleared some of the other debris away, she got at better look at it. It was a painting of an old, drunk-looking donkey, with a zebra-print background and elaborate gilded frame. Patty dusted it off admiringly. "Isn't it charming?"

"Uh . . . sure," she said. "It's a little . . . loud."

"But that's what makes it great. It's quirky. I love it." She shrugged. "So maybe you can find treasures here. What did you get again?"

"A mirror."

"Oh, I bet your mirror wasn't as nice as this. You probably didn't notice it because it was behind all that other junk."

Audrey pointed across the street. "We should probably . . ."

"Right." Patty looked around furtively and then stuck the painting behind another, larger one. "I'll come back and get this later. Fingers crossed no one steals it before then."

"Sure," Audrey said, waiting for her to finish. She carefully concealed the artwork, even sliding a few fake potted plants in front of it so that it would be even harder to find. Meanwhile, Audrey watched the corner where the shooting had taken place. From the porch, there was a clear view of the scene. The police cars that had been there before were now gone.

When Patty was done, the two of them headed for the corner, which was cattycorner from the antiques shop. On the corner, there was nothing more than an old public phone and a streetlamp. No telltale evidence that anything had taken place there.

Audrey scanned the surrounding buildings. The gas station was closest, but there was a CLOSED sign in the window. She looked up, shielding her eyes from the sun. It appeared there was a small apartment upstairs.

"I wonder if anyone up there might've seen anything?" she asked Patty.

"Looks like it's boarded up?"

Audrey squinted. Sure enough, all the windows were covered in boards. "Hmm. I wish we could talk to the person who was working at the gas station."

But that would have to wait. Abandoning that idea, she scanned across to the other side of the street and noticed a small café. There was a sign outside that said *Café Corleone*. It had big picture windows overlooking the street and gas station, and appeared to be a bit of a busy place.

"There. That's our next—"

"Cosa ci fai qui?" a male voice boomed behind them.

They whirled in unison to see two large police officers bearing down on them.

CHAPTER FOURTEEN

The two men approached them cautiously. Audrey stiffened. Patty put an arm on hers. "Let me take care of this," she said. *"Agenti! Ciao!"*

One of them said, "Americans? What are you two Americans doing here?"

So they didn't know who Patty was. Maybe they could use this to their advantage. Patty opened her mouth to speak, but Audrey beat her to the punch. "Yes! We are tourists! Sisters! Fresh from America! We are lost! Can you help us?"

She could feel Patty's eyes on her, questioning.

The two men relaxed, and one rolled his eyes at the other. Then he said, "Where are you trying to get to?"

Thinking quickly, Audrey said, "Well . . . someplace good to eat?"

She winced when he pointed at the Café Corleone behind them.

"Oh! Is that place any good?"

He shrugged. "It's close, at least. Now, ladies, you don't want to be here now. Please move along. This is an active crime scene."

Patty, playing along, said, "A crime scene? What happened?"

The other officer said, "A shooting."

The women gasped in unison. Patty brought her hands to her cheeks. "Oh. That's terrible! Who was shot?"

He held up a hand. "We're working on the details."

"What a terrible crime. Did you catch the criminals?" Audrey asked.

"No, unfortunately. That's why we're here. We're trying to find any witnesses. But so far, we've found nothing."

"Oh!" Patty brought her hand to her forehead. "I don't know if I want to stay here in this town, if it's so riddled with crime!"

The officer shook his head. "I assure you, it's an isolated incident. Corleone is a very safe town. Don't be worried."

"You've really found no witnesses whatsoever?" Audrey asked, her hopes plummeting. If they hadn't found anything, how did she hope to?

"Not yet. But we will. And we're committed to finding out who did this. Now, if you would please move along . . ." He moved closer to them, edging them off the corner.

Audrey looked at Patty, who shrugged. Then they turned around and headed across the street to the Café Corleone.

Inside, the breakfast rush was emptying out. There were only a few occupied tables in the place, which had a small dining room filled with mismatched furniture and old-style flowered wallpaper. There was a pastry case when they walked in, and Patty grinned. "Oh, let's sit. I'm starving, and whatever that is smells so good."

"Didn't you eat at home?" Audrey asked. She hadn't, so she had to admit her stomach was grumbling, too.

"Yeah, but just a piece of bread. And limoncello jam gives me the munchies."

A woman behind the counter grouched something in Sicilian to them. It didn't sound like a welcome. "What did she say?" Audrey whispered to her.

"She said that they're in between breakfast and lunch right now so all they have is what's in the case," then called back to the woman. Audrey translated herself: *That's fine with us, can we sit anywhere?*

A disembodied grunt of a *Si* came from the back of the restaurant. They sat at a table close to the picture window. Audrey drummed her fingers on the paper placemat. When she dipped the horizontal blinds, she could see the crime scene perfectly. The officers were wandering around there, occasionally stooping to look at something or write in a notepad.

"Those guys look about as useless as a three-legged horse," Patty muttered. "Seriously, no wonder Corleone is where the biggest mob bosses of the last century have come from. With a police force like that, they could run amok without any fear of getting caught."

"I can't believe that no one saw anything," Audrey said, looking around. "This isn't Times Square, but it's pretty busy. There have to be some witnesses somewhere."

"You would think," Patty agreed.

"And what time did the guys run in last night? Like, six? That means they were shot at dinnertime. This place had to have been busy. Right?"

Patty nodded.

"So there had to be dozens of witnesses right here. Maybe the waitress can give us some names." She shook her head at the two cops. "I get the feeling they aren't even trying."

"Duh. Yeah, they're not," she said with a shake of her head. "They were probably too busy eating donuts in here."

The waitress came up to their table a moment later, pad at the ready. She was an older woman, her hair in a no-nonsense bun, streaked with gray. She grunted something that sounded like, *What can I get you?*

Patty ordered something, to which the woman rolled her eyes until they landed on Audrey. Audrey shrugged. *"E lo stesso per me, per favore."* The same for me, please.

She wanted to ask the woman some questions, but she turned and walked into the back without a pause.

Audrey leaned forward. "What did I just order?"

"Oh. That yummy little pastry in the case with the chocolate sprinkles and the cream. I don't know what it is."

"Like two thousand calories, probably," Audrey said with a smile. "I saw that one on the way in, too. Looks amazing."

"And of course, a cappuccino. Can't have breakfast in Sicily without a cappuccino, too, right?" she said with a grin.

"Right," Audrey said, though she was already bouncing off the walls with anticipation of talking to the waitress. The questions she had were spinning in her head. She checked her phone and tapped her hands on the table anxiously.

A few moments later, the waitress returned with the pastries and cappuccinos. As she set them on the table, Audrey exchanged a look with Patty and said, *"Scusi, posso chiederti una cosa?"*

Patty nodded and shrugged, confirming her question was passable.

The woman grunted a *Si.*

Audrey nodded at her, asking her to go on. Patty pointed across the street and said something about the incident that had happened there.

The woman nodded again and said, *"Si,"* plus a bit more, but Audrey got lost after that.

"What did she say?"

Patty held up a finger and asked another question. The waitress shook her head and began gesticulating wildly toward the windows. Then she made noises like *Pop pop pop!* and gesticulated some more, with the word *caos.*

Chaos.

Finally, Patty nodded and thanked the woman. The waitress grunted some more and headed back into the kitchen. Meanwhile, Patty sunk her teeth into a big bite of the pastry. "Mmmm. This is as good as it looked," she said, voice muffled because her mouth was full.

Audrey stared at her. "Well? Are you going to tell me what she said?"

Her lips twisted. "Nothing good, unfortunately."

"Really? No one in the café saw anything? I find that hard to believe."

"It's true. She said that unfortunately, the sun sets over there." She pointed. "So it is always shining in the windows at dinnertime. They keep the blinds pulled closed, because if they don't, the place gets really hot and the glare is terrible."

"So the blinds were closed during the shooting?"

Patty nodded. "Yep. They heard the gunshots, though, of course. Five or six of them. And then there was chaos, screaming, shouting, running. Everyone got up and ran to see what was going on, but by the time they opened the blinds, the car had driven away and both shooters and victims were gone."

Audrey stared at her pastry, no longer hungry. "So that means no one saw anything?"

"Not a thing, unfortunately, girl."

"But this place is a busy place. There wasn't anyone in the parking lot, anyone outside who might have—"

"She said she hasn't talked to anyone who saw anything. There are only just rumors."

"Great, seems like on the busiest corner in Corleone, in broad daylight, nobody saw anything."

"Or at least, that's what they're *saying*."

"What do you mean?"

Patty shrugged and looked around her. "Well, think about it. It's *mafia*." She leaned in closely and whispered the word like it was forbidden. "Sure, the mafia isn't as powerful these days as it once was, but it's still there. And people remember. They're scared of it. Around here, they know enough not to stick their noses anywhere near possible mafia hits. People who do that have been known to get them cut off, if you know what I mean."

Audrey groaned. This was proving harder and harder with every passing moment. "I didn't realize I was going to come up against all these roadblocks. Isn't there anyone who would speak?"

"Someone crazy, maybe. With a death wish? Or one of us. That's all. My mom used to say you don't really talk the M-word unless you *are* the M-word. And even then, they speak in code, so no one else can understand."

Audrey let out a big sigh. "Well, that's just great."

She gave Audrey a sympathetic look. "So now what do we do?"

"I don't know."

"Looks like we're back to the drawing board, huh?" she said, polishing off the rest of her pastry.

That wasn't good. They didn't have the time to go back to the drawing board. Audrey sat there, twiddling her thumbs, trying to think of another tack while Patty swallowed the last of her pastry. She pointed to hers.

"Mind if I have that, if you're not going to? I'm so hungry."

Audrey pushed it over to her. "Knock yourself out."

Patty's eyes got big as she dragged it closer. Audrey had to wonder where the tiny girl put all those calories. They probably went to the same place her taste in art had gone. Undoubtedly, Patty would absolutely hate the mirror in the back of Rafael's car. Maybe she could've used some decorating tips from someone like Marco Capaldi. He probably . . .

It suddenly came to her. *You don't really talk the M-word unless you are the M-word.* She practically jumped out of her seat at the thought.

"Marco Capaldi!" she announced. "We need to go to his house and talk to him. Right away."

CHAPTER FIFTEEN

Audrey gripped the steering wheel tightly as the two women idled in the driveway of the villa overlooking the town. She looked up at the place, taking deep breaths to calm herself.

Marco Capaldi had been a nice man when she'd met him earlier.

But back then, she hadn't known he was mafia. And back then, she hadn't been accusing him of being a killer.

No, this would not be fun.

"What's wrong?" Patty asked. She'd popped a piece of pink bubblegum the second she got in the car and had been chewing noisily the whole twenty-minute drive up the harrowingly steep, one-laned gravel road to the villa.

"I'm just thinking . . . if we go in there, we could be walking straight into the house of a murderer."

She shrugged. "And?"

Audrey looked at her, disbelieving.

"Audrey, dear. Carmine Piccolo isn't exactly Saint Peter. You *slept* in the house of a murderer last night."

Oh, she thought. *That's true.*

Still, she'd been on the good side of that particular killer. And while Marco had been nice to her at the antiques shop, she doubted she'd stay on his good side for long once she came in asking questions. "I think we should have a cover."

"A cover?"

She nodded. "We shouldn't just start asking him questions about the shooting, right off the bat." She rubbed her clammy hands together, thinking. "I have an idea. We pretend there's something wrong with our car and ask him for help with it. That way, at least, we can be outside and make a run for it if he tries anything funny."

"Yes! Right. That makes total sense, *Awd.*" She grinned. "You should be a detective. Anyone ever tell you that? If the whole saving-pets thing doesn't work out for you. Or maybe you could combine the two. Be a pet detective, like in that movie?"

Audrey laughed as she got out of the car, facing the house. Before she knew what she was doing, she turned to find Patty standing in front of the open hood of the car, fiddling inside. "What are you doing?"

She pulled her hand out, wiped it on her leggings, and carefully closed the hood. "Well, if you want to have car trouble, you have to be convincing."

Audrey's eyes widened. "But what if you—"

"Relax. My brothers are all mechanics. I just did a little thing. It's nothing."

Now, Audrey was even more worried. What if the car didn't start again? What if they wound up stranded at this rival mafia murderer's home?

She turned to the door. *Remember, he's a nice guy. He's a nice guy. He's a nice guy,* she chanted to herself as she climbed the two slate steps to the front porch. There was an aged bronze knocker the size of Audrey's head on the front door. It was heavy as she lifted it and let it go.

Patty rolled her eyes. "Talk about tacky."

This from a woman who wanted the ugliest painting on Earth? Audrey didn't even have time to complete the thought, though, because a second later, the door opened to reveal a tiny woman in an apron. "*Si?*"

Before Audrey could speak, Patty launched into a long Sicilian monologue, her voice bright and chipper. She motioned to the car in the driveway a lot, so Audrey only hoped she was telling her the story they'd made up.

The woman nodded and said, "*Mi scusi un attimo, per favore.*"

When the woman left, Patty nudged Audrey. "She's his housekeeper-slash-side dish, I bet you."

"Shh. Just act natural. We are here because of the car—"

Patty waved her away. "What do you think? I'm not an amateur. I had the lead in *The King and I* at Newark High's spring musical."

That didn't reassure Audrey as much as she would've liked. Before she could ask more, Marco Capaldi appeared in the doorway. "*Si?*"

Then he looked at Audrey, and his eyes widened with recognition. He wagged a finger at her, as if trying to place her.

"Marco! Hi! It's me, Audrey. From the antiques store?"

"Of course, the American with the mirror! How are you? Did the mirror work out well? I never expected you to show up at my door!"

"This is such a coincidence!" she said, pouring on the sweetness. "So nice to see you again. I have been traveling so haven't tried the mirror out yet. But I will soon! This is my friend Patty from Newark, New Jersey."

He nodded at her, smiling. For a moment, Audrey wondered if he might recognize her. But if he did, he gave no indication. "Pleased to meet you, Patty. The pleasure's all mine—two beautiful American women on my doorstep."

Patty didn't say anything at first. When Audrey looked at her, her expression was the same one a child would have when forced to eat broccoli. So much for being a great actress. She mumbled, "Charmed."

He stepped aside. "Well, I'm sorry for standing here, no manners whatsoever. Come in."

Beside her, Patty bristled.

Audrey pointed outside. "Actually, I was just out on a ride and our car started making a funny noise. I was afraid to drive it, so we stopped at the first house we came to. And it turned out to be yours!"

"Ah?" He poked his head out and looked at the dark sedan. "That's your car?"

Was it her imagination, or was there some disbelief in that question? She nodded. "Yep. All mine."

He stepped outside and closed the door behind him, then began rolling up the sleeves on his starched white dress shirt. "I'm not much of a mechanic, but I will see what I can do."

"Oh, thank you," Audrey gushed. "You have no idea what this will mean to us."

Patty just stood there, mute. Audrey nudged her. "Great," she mumbled. "Thanks."

Audrey led him over to the car and gave him the keys. He opened the driver's side door and sat behind the steering wheel. He turned the key in the ignition. The car sputtered sickly and died. He tried it again with the same result.

"You said it was making a funny noise? It's not working at all anymore. Let's see what's under the hood."

He got out and popped the hood. They followed closely behind him, watching as he said, "Sounded like it could be something with the catalytic converter."

Patty coughed and rolled her eyes, then whispered under her breath, *"So wrong."*

Audrey nudged her again, as Marco looked up at them, a curious look on his face. "So," Audrey said, "you make any good buys in town yesterday?"

He shook his head. "No, I just stopped in to see if there was anything new since the last time I was there, which was only a couple days before. But my real purpose of going down there was meeting with a friend. We have dinner together every Friday night."

"Oh, so you must've been in town for that horrible shooting. Did you hear about it?"

"Yes." He pressed his lips together as he leaned into the car's chassis, testing this thing and that. "Terrible. I think you might have a couple of loose wires here. I'll just tighten them up and see where that gets u—"

"We were surprised, because Corleone seemed like such a quiet town," Audrey went on.

"Oh, it is. Normally."

"Well, we were concerned, vacationing here, only to hear about a shooting so close to where we were staying. It really rattled us. Who do you think could've done something like that?"

He paused, clearly stricken by the question. "No idea."

"No idea?" Audrey asked, leaning forward. "But you've lived here a long time, haven't you? And you were practically on the scene when it happened, right? So—"

He pulled himself upright and studied her. "But that doesn't mean I know anything about the shooting. Why are you asking me this? Who are you?"

"I'm—"

"Your worst nightmare!" Patty shouted, her face red with rage. "Admit it. You're the one who shot them. You killed my Bruno!"

She started to pummel the guy with her fists. He quickly moved to grab them and subdue her, his face flooding with understanding. "*Your* Bruno. You mean, you two are. . . Piccolos?"

Disgust seeped into his features.

"Ha! See?" Patty said triumphantly, still trying to free herself from his hold. "He knew exactly who the victims were. So it was you, Marco Capaldi! Admit it."

He threw her arms down and backed away. "This is ridiculous. I'll admit no such thing. I was in town for the shooting, but I was across the street at the café, having dinner, just like I said." He patted his pockets and pulled out his wallet. "I even have a receipt for it somewhere here.

The blinds were closed. We all saw nothing. By the time we did, it was all over."

"Liar!" Patty said, advancing on him again, fists raised.

He backed away, around the car, but this time, Audrey stepped between them. "Wait. So, Marco, how did you know the victims were Piccolos, then?"

"Word gets around. Besides, I saw Luigi's car pulling off. I figured something had happened to the Piccolos. But as much as I'd have liked to take credit for it, I can't."

Behind Audrey, Patty tensed. "He's lying. He's a lying sack of—"

"Patty. Hold on," Audrey said, turning to her. "Can we please call a truce for a few minutes?"

She scowled at him. "But he killed Bruno."

"I did no such thing!" he shouted back. "Stupid Piccolo clan. Always jumping to the wrong conclusion."

"Idiotic Capaldis," she retorted, sticking out her tongue.

He scowled back and mimicked her, in a childlike, petulant tone.

Oh my God. Are these people for real? I feel like I'm in a kindergarten classroom.

Audrey held up a hand. As easy as it would've been to blame a Capaldi for this murder, to sanction the Piccolo plan to assassinate him, Audrey believed him. His story checked out, and he seemed earnest. It only made her more nervous for the coming deadline—if Marco Capaldi really was innocent, then this was about more than justice—it was about saving a life, making sure a man wasn't sentenced to death for a crime he didn't commit.

Marco regained his composure and said, "I'm going back inside. Your car should be fixed. If you two know what is good for you, you will please leave my property at once."

Audrey stared after him, feeling guilty as she watched him pull open the door to his home. He glanced back at her only once, and in that brief, one-second moment that her eyes met his, she knew exactly what he felt about her. It wasn't anything good.

The least she could do was work to try to keep him alive.

She climbed into the car, and Patty got in beside her, still cursing under her breath. When she turned the key, it started right up.

"Why did you let him get away like that?" Patty complained, still staring at the house with contempt as Audrey eased the car down the steep driveway. "He's so guilty, it's coming out his ears."

"Maybe he's guilty of some things. But I really don't think murdering Bruno is one of them," Audrey said with a shrug. "I believed him. Don't you?"

"No. Not one bit."

"But think about it. If we wanted to confirm, all we needed to do is go down and ask that waitress if he was in the restaurant. He dines there every Friday, so surely the waitress would remember him. If you're going to kill someone, you don't do it at a time and place when you're likely to be there. Do you?"

Her lips twisted. "I guess not."

"I think we need to go back to Cielo d'Azzurro and learn more about who the Piccolos' biggest enemies are, besides the Capaldis."

"Girl, make sure you bring some strong cappuccino. That'll take a long time. They have a lot of enemies."

Audrey shrugged. "It's our best shot right now. My thought is, whoever killed your boyfriend knew that Marco would be there, and thought he could pin it on him. Maybe whoever did this wanted to start a war between the rival families, and knew this would do it."

She nodded. "Okay. That makes sense. But nobody in our family actually *likes* war. They do it because they have to. As a matter of honor. Who would do something so insane as to start it?"

"I don't know," Audrey said. "That's what we need to find out."

CHAPTER SIXTEEN

Audrey and Patty returned to the Piccolo estate in the early afternoon. As Audrey navigated up the gravel drive to the villa, she checked the clock on the dashboard. Just after noon. *Only seven hours left.*

"So you are just going to march into Uncle Carmine's office and ask him to list his enemies?" Patty said, horrified. "You've got guts, girl."

"He's *your* uncle."

"Yes. And he's still terrifying! You've said more to him than I have."

Audrey gave her a doubtful look. "You can't be serious."

"Oh, I am—serious as a heart attack. He's always with that entourage of his, too, so the most I've ever said to him was hello and goodbye. His time is very valuable."

Audrey cringed at her memory of last night, when she'd been discovered snooping outside his office. Good thing she hadn't known how rare it was to get an audience with the don. If she had, she might've done something even more embarrassing, like thrown up on him.

Of course, if she *had* known, she likely would've stayed away from him altogether, and never been put into this awful predicament of trying to prevent a mob war.

"Well, if Rafael is home, maybe I'll just ask him," she said as they pulled into a space near the rest of the black sedans. "If he's been learning everything from his father, he should have a good idea, right?"

"Right," Patty said, waving a hand in front of her face. "Whew. It's hot. I think while you do that, I'm going to get me a glass of lemonade and have a dip in the pool. As long as Sandro isn't in it. *So* gross. Like everyone wants to see him in that little Speedo?"

Audrey only wished she had time to think about such things. But right now, she was a woman on a mission. When she went inside, she followed a trail of thick cigar smoke and found Rafael, sitting at a long, ornate dining table with a number of his mafia brothers—they had their jackets off, sleeves rolled up, and were having a rowdy lunch-slash-strategy meeting. Audrey couldn't understand most of it, since they spoke in rapid-fire Sicilian, but one thing she did understand—*Capaldi*. They said the name over and over again. Which meant one thing.

They had no faith in her. They hadn't stopped planning their hit on Marco Capaldi.

Rafael looked up mid-sentence and saw her, standing in the doorway. *"Uno momento,"* he said to his cousin Rocco as he made his way among the many chairs to her. He took her hand gently and led her out to the hallway. "Hello, Audrey. And how has your morning been?"

"Not good," she groused, pointing toward the dining room. "So you're still going through with the hit?"

He didn't meet her eyes as he nodded. "Audrey. There's nothing you can do. There's nothing anyone can do. When they attack us like that, the only thing we can do is respond—"

"I don't think Marco Capaldi did it."

He looked at her like a child who'd just bitten off far more than she could chew. "I understand. You see the best in everyone. That's what I like about you, Audrey. But—"

"No. I *really* don't think he did it."

"Because you met him one time and he helped you with a mirror. Is that it?" He chuckled, amused. "But—"

"No," she said, growing more annoyed. "I just came from his house and he has an alibi."

His appeasing smile fell. "Wait. You *what?*"

She winced. She hadn't expected to blurt it out like that. "Yes, you see, I stopped by his house and spoke to him."

He pulled a hand down his face and began to speak, stopped, and tried again. "I'm sorry. Did you just say you went to Marco Capaldi's house?"

"Well, I—"

"What in the world were you thinking! You could've been killed. He's a murderer—"

"*You* are murderers, too," she retorted, clenching her hands at her sides.

His face fell. When he spoke next, his voice was quieter. "The Piccolo family may have done some things, but—"

"But you seem to be hearing only what you want to hear. Seeing what you want to see. I just told you Marco Capaldi has an alibi. Do you have any response to that?"

He crossed his arms and snorted. "I doubt it's a good one."

"It can be confirmed by the dozens of people he was with while he was eating at the café across the street. That was where he was. He even has a receipt. You can check it."

He raised a hand to silence her. "Stop. It doesn't matter."

"Why? Why wouldn't it matter? He's the reason—"

He slumped against the wall. "Because one of our own is dead. They're out for blood. It isn't just Bruno. That's the tip of the iceberg. The truth is that our family has been looking for a reason to put an end to this for years, and now they finally have it. They won't listen to reason."

She pursed her lips. "I don't believe that. Just tell me who I have to convince, and I will."

"You know who." He shook his head. "But it's impossible. No one convinces him."

Audrey bristled. She knew he'd say that. Carmine Piccolo. The man everyone lived in fear of, even his own family. "All right. Where is he?"

"In his office."

She turned to march over there, but he grabbed her hand, pulling her toward him, so that she wound up almost flush against him. She blushed and stumbled back, unsure if he'd meant to tug her that hard. Had he? He looked down at her, and for a moment, she thought he might try to kiss her, but then he righted her and said, "You don't have to do this."

"Yes, I do."

"We can figure something else out."

"Like what?"

When he didn't respond, she knew he was out of answers. She pulled himself from his grip and headed for Carmine's office.

"Audrey. Do you want me to go with you?"

She shook her head and squared her shoulders. "Of course not. Unlike everyone else, I'm not afraid of your father."

At least, she didn't want to be. Her stomach churned. Behind her, she could feel Rafael's eyes on her, like *You should be. You don't know what he can do.*

It was a good thing she hadn't eaten anything all day, because throwing up was a definite possibility.

*

Taking a deep breath, Audrey knocked on the heavy wooden door. The sound seemed to echo deep within herself. Her knees wobbled as a voice said, *"Entra."*

She pushed open the door to find the same scene she'd witnessed the day prior: Carmine, at his desk, surrounded by his many frighteningly large bodyguards. He was wearing glasses and poring over some documents. He pulled them off and regarded Audrey as she stepped into the room.

"Audrey Smart. You have news for me?"

She nodded. "Yes, I do."

He motioned her forward. She took a couple of steps, wavering ever so slightly as her feet dug into the plush pile of the thick rug. "And? Don't keep us in suspense."

She scanned the room, trying to keep her dizziness at bay. Everyone was looking at her, waiting for her next words.

"Marco Capaldi is not the shooter," she announced. "He has an alibi."

She might as well have announced that she wanted to be a ballerina when she grew up. The rest of the men went back to whatever they'd been doing. The corners of Carmine's mouth rose in what was probably as close to a smile as he got. He said, "And what alibi does he have?"

"He was in the café across the street, and the blinds were closed. He has a receipt. There are at least a dozen witnesses who could corroborate his—"

"A dozen witnesses that are on the Capaldi payroll," one of the bodyguards behind him said. "I bet—"

Carmine raised a hand, which shut him up at once, but nodded. "Carlo is right. In this town, you are either with us, or against us. It's likely Capaldi bought their silence."

Audrey wanted to sink into that plush rug, never to emerge again. "Oh."

He leaned in. "How did you learn about that?"

"Oh, I um—" Recalling the way Rafael had looked at her when she'd told him about her visit to the Capaldi villa, she coughed. "I went to the café and asked around."

He chuckled, low and mirthless. "Working hard to get me that proof, eh? You're going to have to work a lot harder than that," he said, motioning her off. "Now, if you'll excuse us, we're discussing arrangements for Bruno."

He went back to the document, but she couldn't help but ask. "Arrangements? You mean funeral arrangements?"

"*Si*. And for his family." He didn't look up.

"Where is his family, anyway? Do they know?"

He let out a big sigh and looked up at her, exasperated. "His wife was his only family. And yes. We take care of them the best we can."

Audrey's jaw dropped. "His wife?" she blurted. "But—"

"Yes." He tilted his head at her. "Are we done here? I have a lot of work to do."

She felt as though she'd been slapped across the face. She nodded and stepped away, reeling as she closed the door behind her.

Bruno had a wife. And yet he was seeing Patty. Did she know? And who was this woman? Clearly, she was the one who would inherit, if Bruno were to die. Was there something to that?

In the hallway, she looked around, but Rafael was nowhere to be found. Maybe he didn't want to be witness to whatever he thought his father was going to do to her.

But it wasn't Rafael she wanted to see right now.

It was Patty. Why hadn't Patty told her that her beloved boyfriend was two-timing her?

CHAPTER SEVENTEEN

Still in a daze, Audrey went outside. She found Patty Randazzo sitting on a lounge chair at the edge of the pool, wearing a hot pink bikini, reading an Italian fashion magazine, and sipping on a lemonade as she sunned herself.

As Audrey marched over to her, she noticed Alessandro there, at the pool's edge, talking to her. Luckily, he was in the deep end.

As she approached, he waved at her. "Come to take me up on my offer, I see."

"No," she said flatly.

"Aw, come on! Come on! The water's perfect!" He made a motion like he was going to splash her.

"Don't," Audrey warned, though if he had, she wouldn't have cared much. The heat was oppressive, and there wasn't any shade to be found.

Patty dropped the magazine on her tanned belly and sighed. "Well, once again, Sandro ruins my plans to go in the pool. He's such a little *demon*." She fluffed her over-sprayed curls. "It's so hot, my Aqua Net is melting."

"Come on, you two beautiful ladies! I can handle you both!" he called, stroking through the dark water of the pool. "Cool off with me."

Patty dipped her sunglasses and waved him off. "For the last time, Sandro. I. Am. Your. Cousin!"

"Distant! Very distant!" he called as he swam to the other end of the pool.

She rolled her eyes and muttered, "Never. Ever. Anyhow. Bruno and I used to swim together here. We had so much *fun*." She sniffled. "I can't believe he's gone. He really was the best of men. A true Prince Charming. I'll never meet anyone like him."

Audrey sat on the lounge chair next to her, thinking, *Some Prince Charming. Tell that to his wife.* "Why did you not tell me that Bruno was married?"

From the look in her eyes, this news was not a surprise to her. She said, "He's *not* married."

Now Audrey was thoroughly confused. "He's not? But—"

"Oh, maybe on paper. But not in his heart. That woman—Giada—is a regular witch."

"So you know her? Her name is Giada?"

She nodded. "She lives in downtown Corleone, in the home *he* purchased for her. She was always on his case. She never stopped calling him, wanting to know what he was up to. And get this—sometimes we'd go to town to dinner in the center of town, and she'd catch wind of it and follow us around. Like, even sitting in the same restaurant and just staring at us, for hours."

"Maybe she did that because you were out with her husband?"

"No! The relationship is basically over," Patty said. "He fell out of love with her, told her he wanted a divorce. The papers were in the works. We only started dating once he showed me the papers he had his lawyer draw up. I'm no husband-stealing bimbo, I promise you that. I've got class."

"But she was probably still bitter about it. I think any woman would be."

"*Awd,* you don't get it. I understand, feeling betrayed. He doesn't want her anymore. That's gotta sting. But she went overboard. She was like, full-on stalker mode! When she saw us at dinner, after watching us for hours, she attacked us! With a dinner knife! When the waiter held her back, she told me she was going to get me! She's insane!" She gesticulated wildly.

Audrey let out a disbelieving laugh. Mentally imbalanced, living in town, standing to inherit all of the deceased's money . . . How could Patty keep such a promising lead a secret? She clapped her hands. "You know what this means, right?"

Patty sucked on the straw of her lemonade until the glass was empty. Then she said, "That an insane woman is going to inherit all of Bruno's money, his house in Corleone, everything?" She pouted. "Sad that a witch like that wins. She doesn't deserve it."

"Right . . . but it also means that she has a motive for murdering him. And if she lives in town . . ."

Patty pulled off her sunglasses. "You think she shot Bruno?"

Audrey shrugged. "There's a chance."

"But Luigi . . ."

"Maybe that was an accident. He got caught in the line of fire."

Her jaw dropped. "Oh, my *gawd*, that makes sense! She totally could've gone off her rocker and done that. She was halfway there already. Girl, I don't know why I never thought of that!"

Audrey smiled. "You know where she lives?"

"Do I know where she lives? What kind of question is that! Of course I do! I Google-mapped their house in Corleone the first time I met Bruno," she said with a grin, scooting forward on the lounge chair and scuffing into her hot pink, furry kitten heels. "Come on, I'll take you there. I'd love to give that witch a piece of my mind for taking my Bruno from me!"

Audrey could just imagine the screaming catfight. "Well, hold on. She's a suspect only. We don't know for sure that—"

"Don't tell me you're leaving me?" a voice called from the pool.

Sandro. He was still swimming back and forth, this time in breaststroke, pouting at them. Audrey shrugged. "Sorry!"

"Maybe this evening? We swim at night?"

"Right, Sandro," Patty said, rolling her eyes as she followed Audrey into the house. "How about never? Seriously, though. This is the best lead we've had, Cagney. Let's get our butts in gear!"

Audrey agreed. They didn't have a moment to lose. They had to find this Giada person as soon as possible.

*

The town of Corleone was situated among hills, so the streets went up and down them at precarious angles. Patty directed Audrey to a place she called Piazza Nasce, with a small fountain and cobblestone streets that reminded her of Mussomeli. Here, too, there seemed to be a Catholic church on every corner. She followed Patty's directions up a quaint side street a few blocks from the site of the shooting, past brightly colored row houses lined up next to one another, each slightly higher than the next, like dominoes.

"That's it. That's the one. The yellow one," Patty said, pointing to a small, narrow home sandwiched between others.

Audrey navigated to the side of the street a few houses away from the home and cut the engine, all the while looking up at the house. It wasn't one of the nicer homes on the block. The shutters were pulled tight and the paint was peeling in large swaths, revealing the crumbling plaster underneath. There were no flowers in the many terra cotta pots outside, and the front door had a gash in it, like it had been kicked in.

She looked at Patty as she opened her door. "I think you should stay here."

Patty frowned. "Why?"

98

Wasn't it obvious? "Well . . . you two have a bit of a history. And . . ." *You nearly murdered Marco Capaldi with your bare hands when you thought he'd killed Bruno.*

She shrugged, pulled down the visor, and checked her reflection in the mirror. "Fine, fine. Whatever. I'll just wait here and be bored half to death, baking in the hot sun."

A little dramatic, but Audrey had other things to worry about. She slammed the door and headed up the three wide steps to the tiny porch. She rang the doorbell, hoping that the woman spoke English.

The woman who answered was nothing like Audrey expected. She thought maybe she'd find a clone of Patty. After all, Patty was a definite *type*, the kind of woman it took a certain man to appreciate. But the woman who answered the door was slim and refined, young, with a low, blonde bun and pale skin. She was naturally pretty, without much make-up. "*Si?*"

"Giada?"

The woman nodded.

"Scusami. Parli inglese?"

"Yes," she said, sounding a bit annoyed. "I went to school in Canada. What do you want?"

Audrey gnawed on the inside of her cheek before deciding it was best to just come out with it. "I have bad news for you. It seems that your—"

She waved her hand in the air. "Oh, if this is about Bruno, I know already. The police were already here."

"You know? You don't seem very broken up about it."

She laughed bitterly and started playing with a loose thread on the sleeve of her cardigan. "Well, why should I be? He was a snake. A scoundrel."

"What happened between you two?"

"It's more like, what *didn't* happen between us? I knew him all my life. I thought he was a good man. When I came back from Canada after school, he told me he had a job that paid well. I thought he was a salesman. Little did I know that he'd gotten himself involved with those terrible Piccolos." She shook her head in disgust. "They murder and steal and do all types of terrible things. He was gone all the time. And then I find out he has an American mistress."

"He hurt you."

With a single, violent motion, she ripped the thread of her cardigan out, opening a little hole in the fabric. She ignored it. "Yes. Worse than anyone. I gave my youth, all of my love. And he treated it like it was garbage. He walked all over me. So no, I can't say I care that he's dead. Actually—" She thought for a moment. "I do care."

"You do?"

"He was stupid with money. Throwing it around like crazy on stupid things to make himself seem more important than he was. Spending it all on that American floozy. But he had a little bit saved. This house was all his. And now it is all mine. So *that's* what I care about." She gave a cold, indifferent shrug. Then her eyes narrowed. "Who are you?"

"I'm a . . ." Audrey looked around, her eyes fastening on a metal star attached to the wall. "I'm a reporter with *The Star*."

"*The Star*? I've never heard of that."

"Yes. It's a mostly online publication, but we have universal reach," Audrey fudged quickly. "We're doing a feature on whether the mob still exists today. What are your thoughts on that?"

She snorted. "It does. Bruno could've told you that. And probably whoever did me a favor by shooting him."

"Where were you when you heard about the shooting?" she asked.

"Well, I was in town, actually. I even heard the shooting myself."

"Really? What were you doing in town?"

"Oh, I was on the street, heading down to the Café Corleone. I was just on my way there when I heard the shots. It made me jump!" She shuddered. "I went running to see what was going on, and that's when I saw a car speeding away. I didn't realize it was Bruno until afterwards, when the police came to my door."

"So you were alone, then, when the shooting occurred? You don't have anyone to corroborate your story?"

She frowned. "No. I was meeting up with someone at the café. I ran to the café after that and found them all standing outside, watching the scene."

"You were meeting someone . . ." Audrey muttered, thinking. That sounded awfully familiar. "A man?"

She smiled. "Yes."

"Marco Capaldi?"

The woman blinked, and her eyes got a little dreamy. "That's right. How did you know?"

"I interviewed him and he said he was meeting a friend, so I just put two and two together." She shifted on the stoop, thinking. "You do know that Marco Capaldi is mafia as well, don't you?"

She nodded. "Or so I hear. But really, their family is trying to get out of it. They want peace. It's people like Bruno and his clan who want to stir the pot. They are evil. *Evil*. His new girlfriend is one of them. A disgusting Piccolo." She spat at Audrey's feet. "They're the worst of the worst. I am sure it was one of the other mafia clans that did this to them, and good for them! I'd be happy if the Piccolos were all wiped off the map."

"Really?" Audrey said, a little shocked by this refined, demure woman's hatred of the family. "So is that who you think did it?"

"Probably. There are other, smaller clans. And Bruno was a gambler. I bet he stole from one of them or something. And so he finally cashed in his chips. The others can go straight to hell with them. They're no better."

"Why do you say that?"

She shook her head. "Anyone in town could tell you! I have heard plenty more stories about that family. Why he got involved with them is beyond me. I only wish I'd known it before I married him. But Marco knows, he'll tell you. The Capaldis were innocent, just trying to run their business, but it was the Piccolos who did vile things, trying to put them out of business. It was terrible, twenty years ago. Did you know Carmine Piccolo murdered Marco's grandfather in cold blood?"

Audrey stared. "No!"

"Oh, yes. They want to rule this town, and will stop at nothing. Nothing!" She pointed at Audrey. "Write that in your story. I'm not afraid to show myself to them. Would you like a picture of me? I have one, if you—"

"No, that's not necessary. But that's very brave of you. I hear most people wouldn't want to get in the way of the Piccolos."

"I don't care. I've had enough of them. They can kill me if they want. I spit on them! Every one of them!" The woman studied her. "You don't look like a reporter. Did you record our conversation?"

Audrey nodded and lifted her phone and lied, "Yes. It's all in here."

"All right," she said warily, moving to close the door. "Is there anything else you would like to know?"

Audrey pretended to think. "No, I think that's it. I appreciate your time."

She went to step backwards and return to her car, but the woman stiffened and suddenly yelled, "You!"

Audrey's eyes shot to Giada, who threw open the door and flew down the steps, headed straight for Patty, who was standing in the street, taunting her with rude hand gestures.

Audrey rolled her eyes before breaking into action and rushing down the stairs. A storm was coming. She could feel it.

CHAPTER EIGHTEEN

Audrey didn't have time to catch up with Giada. She wasn't sure she could do anything, even if she had. The two forces struck one another with such violence, Audrey could only skid to a stop and stare. They started to go at it, all fingernails and fangs, shrieking and scraping at one another. Patty got ahold of the woman's bun somehow, loosening it, and suddenly, hair was flying wildly about as they screamed and cursed one another.

Audrey tried to put herself between the two women, but she only managed to get a handful of hair and an elbow to her jaw. "Ow!" she cried, backing away.

"You witch!" Patty shouted, her face red. "You killed my Bruno!"

Audrey looked at the sky. Not this again. Clearly, Piccolos had a temper problem, which was probably why they were known for all this violence.

"Patty!" Audrey shouted.

That did no good. They continued scraping and clawing at one another. At one point, Patty got Giada in a headlock and tossed her to the ground, then jumped on top of her. Then she started pummeling her with her fists.

"Patty! Stop!" Audrey cried as the woman underneath her put up her hands to defend herself, moaning.

She clamped a hand on Patty's shoulder and yanked her arm back before she could deliver another blow.

"Let me go! Let me kill her!" Patty growled. "She took my Bruno from me! He was too good for her. She ruined everything."

"Patty," Audrey said evenly, finally getting her to stand up and stagger off Giada. "She has an alibi."

By now, a small crowd had gathered. Giada rolled to her side, breathing hard, and sat up. Her lower lip was bleeding, her blonde hair in her ruddy face.

"What kind of alibi?" Patty muttered, still giving Giada the death-glare.

"Well, it turns out, she's dating Marco Capaldi," Audrey said, then wondered if she should've.

103

"She's *what*?" Patty's eyes got big. "The stinkin' traitor! I should've known! Bruno was right about you!"

She rushed forward to give Giada another kick, but Audrey managed to grab her by the strap of her halter top and keep her back. "Come on. I'll tell you the rest later."

Giada crawled to her hands and knees and stood up. She started shouting in Sicilian to Patty, and Patty retorted with more arm gestures. Audrey didn't want to translate—she had a good enough idea what they were saying to each other. More people began popping out of the homes on the street to see what was going on. Audrey blushed as she dragged Patty back to the car.

When they were back inside, Patty sighed. "She's a total witch. I told you. How Bruno could ever be interested in a girl like her . . . I'll never know."

"Hmm," Audrey said, thinking. She pulled away from the curb and left the commotion behind.

"Hmm? Is that all you have to say? You saw her! Isn't she hideous? No fashion sense whatsoever."

"Yes," Audrey said, employing her *Never say no to a Piccolo* motto. "Totally."

"And I can't believe she's going with Marco Capaldi," she said, shaking her head. "Actually, I totally can believe it! They're both scum! The bottom of the barrel! The both of them! They belong together. And may they rot in hell with the rest of the Capaldi family."

"But that's the thing. I saw the way she looked when I mentioned Marco. I think she's really in love with him. When did that stalking incident you mentioned happen?"

Patty shrugged. "I don't know. It was when we were first together. Two months ago."

"So I don't know. To me, it seems like she might have moved on."

"So?"

"So, if she had, why would she want to kill Bruno?"

"Duh. The money. She and Marco were probably in it together."

"But she and Marco were meeting for a date. I don't think it's logical that she would see Bruno in a place he usually isn't at, shoot him, and then go to her date. Does that sound plausible to you?"

Patty's lips twisted. "Well, no. But neither does anything any of them does. They're stupid. They behave stupidly. I still think they could've done it, no matter what anyone says."

104

That was true. Maybe the Capaldis had, and had paid off all the witnesses, like Carmine said.

And in that case, maybe the hit was justified.

But she still didn't want to believe it.

Still, as she drove, she had to admit they were at another dead end. And now it was just after two. Less than five hours, and Carmine would order that hit.

She pressed on the gas, urging the car to go faster.

*

When Audrey and Patty returned to the Piccolo estate, everything was quiet. It felt like the calm before the storm, as if everyone was holding their breaths for something terrible that was about to come.

A little ray of sunshine arrived when Audrey stepped to the front door and Nick popped his head out from among the bushes. "There you are, Bub," she said, smiling. "Did you have a good time exploring?"

He stared at her expectantly, as if to say, *Please feed me.*

"All right, all right, let's go inside," she said to him, scooping him up and hurrying inside, behind Patty.

Patty tapped her chin. "What are the chances Sandro has evacuated the pool area and will leave me in peace? It's after two and I need to get that swim in before the sun goes down!"

"If he's still in the pool, he's probably a prune by now," Audrey said.

Patty looked around. "I wonder where everyone is. I bet they're planning and plotting. . ."

That made Audrey's heart thump. If they were planning, she knew what. And it could only end badly for everyone involved.

Together, they went to the kitchen, where Nick suddenly jumped from her arms. He hissed. Pickle yipped. Then, without warning, they started chasing each other in exhausting circles, a small animal tornado.

"Stop!" Audrey cried. She didn't have time for this. She dared to reach into the melee and pick Nick up, but not before he swiped a paw across her forearm, leaving a long red scratch. "Ouch."

She pulled back and looked at the injury, which began to bubble with blood. "Great."

Patty managed to get Pickle in her arms, putting an end to the commotion, as Audrey ran the injury under the faucet. "Thanks, Bub," she said to the fox. "I was going to give you something special, but forget it now. Out."

She pointed out the window. The fox whimpered, then turned and followed her finger, disappearing out the window. As he did, her wound began to sting. She blotted at it with some paper towel, groaning, then fished out her phone.

It had blown up with messages and texts. She'd expected some from Concetta, and she had a few, just checking in to say that things at the vet center were quiet. But she also had some messages from Mason, starting from the previous night.

Hey. Stopped by to see you. You okay?

She smiled at that, but her spirits took a nosedive when she read the rest of his messages, starting earlier this afternoon:

Hey. Nessa just came by. She said there's water coming out your front door.

Water? Had she forgotten to turn off a faucet somewhere? Had a pipe burst?

Guess you're not here. So you went.

She frowned. Was it just her, or did he sound bitter?

Got inside and shut it down. Upstairs toilet overflowed.

Well, that was a relief that he took care of it. Still, she needed to get back. Who knew what kind of mess waited for her?

Forgetting her injury, she quickly dialed Mason's number. He answered with a "Well, if it isn't the missing veterinarian, back from the dead. Where you been?"

"Hi, Mason. Sorry. I've been busy here. I got your text. I—"

"So, how are the mafia? They accept you into their fold yet?"

Once again, she sensed a bitterness behind his teasing lilt. She didn't have time for that. "They're fine. How is my house. Is it that big of a mess?"

"Not too bad. Nessa and I've been cleaning up for the last two hours, though. We had to put your rugs out to dry on the back patio but I don't think there'll be any lasting damage."

"Nessa?" Her stomach sank. The thought of those two perfect people together made her feel ill.

"Well, she was here at first, at least. But then she got a call from her agent and disappeared."

That sounded more like Nessa. "It's a good thing she told you. Thank you for getting in. How did you do that, by the way?"

"Picked the lock. Wasn't hard."

106

"I didn't know you had a criminal background."

"Not nearly as much as your present company," he said, and there was definite bitterness in his voice this time. "When you gettin' back? Soon, right? It's Sunday night. You'll probably need to get a plumber in here. I fixed it for now, but it's running kind of weird and making me think you might have a blockage in one of the pipes that should be addressed sooner rather than later."

She winced. She knew she should drop everything and have Rafael drive her back. But she couldn't. Not with this mystery unsolved. "Actually, do you know of any? I—"

"Let me guess. You're having too much fun with that smooth mob guy. Got it."

That wasn't it at all. "No, it's—"

"Are you ever coming back?"

"Of course I am. I'll definitely be back tomorrow." *Whether or not I've prevented this mob war. I hope.*

"All right. I know a guy in town. I'll call him and see if he can stop by tomorrow. Take care of yourself, Boston."

"Okay, Mason. Th—"

She realized she was speaking to dead air. He'd hung up on her.

And she probably deserved that. She'd gone on a trip with a good-looking mobster, leaving him to clean up her mess, and she couldn't even come back to take it off his hands. He probably had every right to be upset with her.

Sighing, she turned around and realized she was alone in the kitchen. Everyone had cleared out. Wandering to the center island, she lifted herself up onto a stool, put her elbows on the cool granite counter, and buried her face in her hands.

Four and a half hours, and the mafia would attack Marco Capaldi. No, he wasn't an innocent man. But he was innocent of *this*. That, she was sure of.

Maybe she shouldn't have cared. If she asked Rafael to take her home, he would, and she could simply wash her hands of the whole matter.

But that wasn't her. It wasn't in her nature to stand by and let people get hurt. If she saw a way to prevent it, she had to take action.

Was there a way? She squeezed her eyes closed, trying to think.

Maybe I just need to try to convince Carmine to see that Capaldi couldn't have done this, she thought. *Maybe that's my only choice.*

She was about to slide off the stool and go in search of him when someone gently took her wrist.

She looked up and found Rafael standing above her, staring at her wound. He tsked. "This looks bad."

"It's nothing."

"Well, it may be nothing, but you are the doctor, always taking care of everyone else. Let me at least take care of this for you?"

She relented, letting him pull her toward the sink. The paper towel she'd clamped over the wound was inadequate; it was drenched in blood. He gently guided her forearm under the warm spray of water, then reached underneath the cabinet and pulled out a first aid kit.

Sitting her down, he said, "I wonder if it needs stitches."

She shook her head. "It's already starting to clot. It's fine."

"Stop being the doctor for a moment," he said, squeezing some antiseptic ointment onto a cotton ball. "This may sting."

It wouldn't, Audrey knew, and it didn't. It wasn't alcohol-based. But she decided to allow him to play doctor, since he seemed to enjoy doing it. He gently blew on the antiseptic to dry it, making her skin tickle, and then added a large bandage.

"Good as new."

She smiled. "Thank you."

He held onto her arm almost a beat too long, so that when she looked at him, it seemed impossible to doubt his intentions. He cared about her. But he didn't make any moves to kiss her, just stood there holding her hand. "You're a very impressive woman, Audrey," he said. "We all think so."

"That's not true. I haven't been able to find out anything about the shooting."

He pressed his lips together. "It's all right. None of us thought you would."

"But Capaldi really didn't do it. I'm sure of it. And if he didn't, it stands to reason that someone else did. Don't you care?" Audrey asked, pulling her arm away.

"Of course I care. I—"

"You don't act like it."

He frowned. "What is that supposed to mean?"

"Well, Marco Capaldi has an alibi. Why don't you tell your father? Make him see? He won't listen to me. You're his son. You're probably the only person whose opinion matters."

"It doesn't."

"How do you know?"

He was silent for a moment, but then he shook his head. "I know. I know how it seems." He looked away, and when his eyes met hers, he seemed smaller. "I have always fought against my father. Taken a gentler approach. He never liked it. That's why he threatens me every so often, to hand everything over to Sandro. But I can't let Sandro take the reins. If I do, he'll kill himself and everyone else in the family. My little brother doesn't think. He jumps into things without using his head."

"He thinks you're weak."

Rafael nodded. "Yes, very. He's wanted to bring Marco down for a long time, and this is his chance. If I go against him now, it might be the final nail in the coffin that is our relationship, I fear."

"You don't want to kill Capaldi," Audrey observed.

"No. I don't want to kill anyone. I want all this to stop," he said, shaking his head.

"So how does it stop?" Audrey asked.

"I don't know. If we knew who the killer was, if we had the person in our hands, and we could say here he is, this is the man who shot Bruno, that would satisfy him, I think. He needs to show that when we were attacked, the Piccolo family responded. Justice was served."

She straightened and checked her phone. She still had four hours. "Okay, well . . . we still have time. I'll keep looking."

He raised an eyebrow. "Where are you going to look?"

She fisted her hands at her sides, her mouth pressed into a grim line of determination. "I don't know. I'll think of something." She rubbed her hands together. "Where is Luigi? Do you think I can ask him some questions?"

"He's . . . out on the patio, getting some sun," Rafael said, motioning toward the door. "By all means, you may. But we already asked him for his version of the story, and you heard it—didn't you?"

He eyed her suspiciously. She shrugged, embarrassed. "Okay, yes. I did. Slightly. As much as I could from out in the hallway. But there might be something I missed."

CHAPTER NINETEEN

Rafael pulled open the door to the back patio. Right away, she saw Luigi, sitting in a lounge chair under the shaded portico. He was wearing dress pants and a dress shirt, the regular uniform, except his shoes were off and his arm was in a sling. He looked miserable as he stared out at the dark blue waters of the lagoon pool.

"Luigi!" Rafael called, to which he turned his head. "How are you? Can I get you anything?"

"Eh," he muttered, waving his hand in front of him to say *so-so*.

Rafael went to the table, where there was a pitcher of ice water, and poured him a glass. Then he poured one for Audrey. "You remember Audrey? She'd like to ask you some questions."

Luigi wasn't exactly welcoming. He looked at Audrey and muttered, *"Per che cosa? Non voglio."*

Rafael crossed his arms. "Luigi," he said in a warning tone. *"Zitto. Non essere così maleducato."* He looked at Audrey. "Make yourself comfortable. My cousin, he will be happy to answer any of your questions. And if he isn't, make sure you let me know about it."

Luigi frowned and motioned to the seat across from him. "What can I do for you, Dottore?"

She sat on the very edge of the seat and said, "Well, I was hoping you could tell me a little bit about what happened yesterday, when you were shot?"

He rolled his eyes. "I thought I already did this."

Rafael barked, "Luigi. *Smettila.*"

Luigi sucked in a breath, then took his time letting it out. "Fine. What do you want to know about it?"

"Just . . . everything. Can you start with when you arrived in town?"

He shrugged. "Yeah, well, I picked up Bruno around four-thirty from his place in Palermo. We made it into Corleone at around five but I needed to juice up my car, so we stopped at the station closest to Cielo d'Azzurro."

"Did you see anyone there while you were getting gas?"

"No. No one." He glanced briefly at Rafael. "Then we parked there because I needed to run an errand for the don down the street."

110

This was news to Audrey. She couldn't remember hearing this before. Maybe somewhere within it was information that could help point her in the direction of a different killer.

"An errand?"

"Nothing illegal, *cara*. Don't look at him that way! He's a good boy, my step-nephew Luigi. *Most* of the time." He winked at Luigi.

"Step-nephew?" Audrey frowned.

"Yes. He's my aunt's—my mother's older sister's—stepchild from her first marriage."

"I have to say, I am so confused by your family tree. I thought Luigi was your cousin."

He shook his head. "I'll draw it out for you some day. Anyway, he was just picking up some stuff from someone in town," Rafael added. Then he leaned over and rubbed Audrey's shoulder. "I'm sorry, I must go. My father expects me to help him with some additional errands."

She watched him walk off, noting the irony of it. So what if the errands Luigi and Bruno were performing weren't illegal on that day? They were involved in illegal doings. They were planning to murder a man. They were far from innocent. So she had every right to look at them any way she pleased.

She turned to Luigi. "So you performed these errands . . ."

"*Si*. So we were on our way, got the stuff, maybe no more than ten minutes."

"You didn't see anyone you knew while you were there? In that busy intersection?"

He shook his head. "Saw lots of people. No one important. No one I cared to remember."

"But people would remember you, though."

He smiled. "I suppose they do."

"You and the Piccolos are known throughout town."

"Yes, I suppose it is true. Our reputation precedes us."

"Okay. And then what happened, after you ran your errand?"

"We were walking single-file on the side of the road, on our way back to the car. We'd just gotten to the corner where the gas station was. And that's when it happened."

"Someone came by and started shooting?"

He nodded. "I heard the first gunshot. Sailed right over my head and hit Bruno right between the shoulder blades. He was a little bit in front of me and went over. When I turned, that's when I got it, in the shoulder."

"You heard only those two shots?"

He nodded, then reached into the front pocket of his shirt and pulled out a small, misshapen piece of black metal, no bigger than a dime. As he held it up to her, she realized what it was.

"That's the bullet?"

He nodded proudly. "The doc took it right from my shoulder. Missed the bone by a millimeter. My first bullet. It's kind of a rite of passage in my line of business."

Audrey gritted her teeth. That was one rite of passage she'd be happy never to experience. "Very nice. So, what happened then?"

"I ran to Bruno. He was bleeding a lot, but he told me we had to get out of there. So I helped him up, got him to our car, and we took off for Cielo d'Azzurro." He shrugged. "That's all."

"Yes, but did you see anything about the person who was shooting at you? What car were they driving?"

He shook his head. "Whoever it was, he wasn't in a car."

Audrey stared at him, confused. "I thought he was? I thought I . . ." She trailed off, thinking. She thought she'd heard it somewhere, but maybe she'd just assumed. Just like the Piccolos had assumed the Capaldis had to have been involved. "Then how did he get away?"

"I don't know. I turned, and I didn't see anyone. Might've been shooting from one of the windows. I saw nothing. Nobody."

Audrey looked at Rafael, stunned. "And no one else saw this? You said there were a lot of people around . . ."

"Yes. They all fell to the ground when the shots were fired."

"And you saw no one there that you knew? No one at all?"

He shook his head. "Well . . . other than Flavio. He was out on the porch, sweeping. I waved at him, he waved back. That was right before the shooting."

"Flavio . . . you mean the shopkeeper at the antiques place?"

Luigi nodded. "That's right."

Audrey straightened. Hadn't Flavio said he'd been inside? That he hadn't seen anything? Was he lying? And if so, why?

"What are you thinking?"

Audrey broke from her thoughts to find Luigi staring at her curiously. "I'm thinking that there may be other witnesses in town that the police haven't talked to."

He shrugged. "What's the difference? The Capaldis are responsible. That's all there is to it. As far as I am concerned, you are wasting your time, and mine."

112

"Maybe so." But it was a lead. A small one, but a lead, nonetheless. And she wouldn't feel right until she checked it out.

She stood up. As she did, Patty scuffed out the doors in her kitten heels, wearing her bikini and a sheer black kimono, carrying her magazine. "Finally!" she shouted, pumping her fist. "Sandro is nowhere in sight. Pool, you are mine! All mine!"

She skipped toward the lounges on the sunny part of the patio, beside the pool. Audrey thanked Luigi, who mumbled a "No problem," and hurried toward her.

She reached Patty just as she was pulling off her kimono. "I have to go back to town."

Patty stared at her. "You got the munchies for one of those pastries from the Corleone Café, too, did you? Girl, I wish they had DoorDash around here; I'd totally get a dozen delivered."

"No. Actually . . ." She looked back at Luigi, who was staring sullenly into the water, ignoring them. "I think I might have a little bit of a lead. I need to check it out."

"No kidding. What?"

"Flavio. At the antiques shop. I think he was lying."

She reached for her kimono. "I can't let you go alone, Cagney. That would make me a bad partner." She scuffed back into her heels. "Plus, I totally forgot that darling painting. I need to go pick it up."

Audrey didn't want to wait, but she also didn't want to face Flavio, who didn't speak a word of English, without a good translator.

"All right. Can you get changed quickly?" she asked, checking her phone. "I don't have much time—"

Patty waved a hand at her. "Oh, forget it. I'll just go like this. I'm decent, right? No problem."

Audrey stared at her. She was decent, but just barely. That bikini left very little to the imagination. "You sure? I can just—"

Just then, the door from the house opened, and Sandro appeared, smiling wolfishly. "Ah! My two American loves!" he shouted. He reached for the hem of his shirt and started to pull it up over his head. "I knew you could not keep away from me for long. Now we have fun, yes?"

"No!" Audrey returned, averting her eyes from the sight of his naked chest.

"Go. Lead the way," Patty muttered, shooing her forward. "Let's get out of here before he takes it all off. I really want to see what Mr. Shopkeeper has to say."

CHAPTER TWENTY

Audrey kept checking the clock on the dashboard as she and Patty drove the convertible into town. She had just over three hours before the deadline. She shifted in her seat, feeling a tightness in her throat that refused to go away, no matter how many times she swallowed.

"I always knew that old shopkeeper was a shifty one," Patty said as they drove, inspecting her claw-like fingernails.

"Really?" Audrey asked. All she'd seen was a slightly grumpy, slightly hard-of-hearing old man. But maybe her impression had been off.

"It was in his eyes. You could tell. He's the kind of snoop who listens at doors and is in everybody's business," she said with a shrug. "When I lived in *Nork*, an old guy just like him lived in the apartment just 'cross the hall. Constantly into my private life. Like seriously . . . *demented*."

"You mean dementia?"

"No. Well, maybe he blamed it on that, but he was just *demented*." She spun a finger by her head. "Insane."

"That's awful."

"Went through my mail! Can you believe it? Old people don't have anything better to do, so they have to butt into everyone else's life. It's the truth. So when this shopkeeper guy said he didn't see anything, I called B.S. right away." She sighed. "Maybe *he* did it?"

Audrey shrugged, though she really couldn't see that slow, stooped man picking off targets across the street like some kind of sharpshooter. "Who knows. I guess we'll find out."

They reached the intersection where the shooting had taken place. Patty motioned to the side of the road, in front of the gas station. "Park here."

Audrey eased the car into the spot and stepped out of the car, then walked to the corner. The police had put crime scene tape around the area. Patty scuffed over to the area in her kitten heels and used her hand to shade her eyes from the setting sun.

"Yep. Yep. Yep. Just as I thought, *Awd*." She pointed cattycorner across the street, toward the shop. "There's a perfect view from the porch of the antiques shop to the scene of the crime."

Audrey nodded and thought about what Luigi said. "Yes. And Luigi said that they were coming back from running an errand near the shop. So their car was probably parked here—" She jumped over to the side of the curb where she imagined the car would be. "And they were coming this way, their backs to him, *here*." She scuttled along to the place where they'd have been if they were walking away from the shop. "Like this. Luigi said Bruno was shot in the back, and when he turned, he was shot in the shoulder."

Patty nodded. "So that means—"

"The shooter wasn't driving a car, and no one seemed to notice them. So it means that the shooter must've been posted somewhere near the antiques store . . ." She squinted as she looked across the street. There was a thick wooden fence, at least five feet high, around the perimeter of the property. There were bushes studded around it at regular intervals, as well. "The shooter might've been behind the fence. Or hidden by the bushes. Or—"

"Or on that second floor!" Patty said, excited. "I told you. That Flavio guy is guilty as sin! Anyone who hoards junk like that has to have a screw loose."

"I think we should probably talk to him before we make that assumption," Audrey said, taking a step in the direction of the shop. As she did, a thought struck her. She stopped abruptly.

Patty bumped into her, nearly sending her stumbling into the street. As she righted herself and turned, Patty said, "What's wrong?"

She paused, trying to determine how best to phrase her next request. "Just that . . . can we proceed gently?"

Patty's brow wrinkled. "What do you mean?"

"Just that the last time I interviewed someone, you two wound up in a catfight in the middle of the street. And the time before that wasn't much better." She shrugged. "So maybe don't go accusing anyone of anything prematurely. Okay? Let me handle that."

Patty raised her eyes to the sky. "Girl. I am usually discretion itself. You just caught me on a bad day. I'm emotional because of Bruno."

Audrey gave her a sympathetic smile. "I understand. But if we're going to catch Bruno's killer, we need to keep a level head, right?"

"Yeah, I guess." She glowered. "If I ever do find the person, I'm going to unleash all my Sicilian American Princess rage upon them, let me tell you that, and it ain't gonna be pretty."

Audrey didn't doubt it.

But *if*. That was the operative word.

She turned to take another step toward the store when she spotted two dark forms across the street. It was the cops she'd seen earlier in the day.

"If it isn't our two American friends," one of them said, smirking as they approached.

They both seemed entranced by the hot pink bikini Patty was wearing, but she made no move to pull her kimono tighter over her body. She said, "Well, hello, Officers. Have you gotten any further in your case?"

They shook their heads. "Unfortunately, no. But we're working through leads and asking questions."

"No? Oh, that's a shocker," she said in mock surprise, giving Audrey a wink. She gave the nearest one a playful punch. "Well, keep at it. We have faith in you."

She grabbed Audrey by the sleeve and started to move past them when one of the officers called, "One of the biggest questions is why two American ladies keep showing up at the scene of the crime."

The two women froze. Patty turned first. "Well, isn't it obvious?" She smiled, batted her eyelashes, then reached out and touched the man on his silver nameplate. "It's usually where the big, strong, brave, *single* cops hang out. I absolutely love a man in uniform."

The older of the two men didn't seem to buy it, because he coughed and grunted. But the younger one, the one she'd touched, looked down at her hand on his chest, and the corner of his mouth quirked up in a smile. "Yeah? What's your name, *bella*?"

She started to speak to him in Sicilian, very flirtatiously, and then giggled. He chuckled. Meanwhile, Audrey checked her phone. Under three hours. That noose around her neck seemed to tighten.

"Well," she announced loudly, pointing at the shop. "I saw something at that antiques store that I really want to pick up, so this is where I leave you!"

She headed off, marching across the street, sweat trickling down her temple. When she reached the other side of the street, she turned to find Patty rushing to catch up with her.

"Sorry! I got a little carried away," she said with a smile, glancing back at the cops, who were still watching them. "But that officer's kind of cute, isn't he?"

Audrey hadn't noticed. She shrugged as they walked the rest of the way to the antiques shop.

"He reminds me a little of Bruno, even. You know, like the shiny side of a coin. Can you imagine—the ultimate tale of forbidden love! Mafia princess and a cop. I think I read a really hot romance novel about that once." She giggled. "Just think about it! Me with a police officer! Carmine would *freak*. Bruno would be rolling over in his grave!"

He's not even in *his grave yet,* Audrey thought as they reached the porch. When they did, Audrey turned. Sure enough, the view of the crime scene from this vantage point was perfect.

Patty waved at the cop, who waved back. Then she went to the place where she'd hidden that hideous painting. No surprise, it was still there. She lugged it out and carried it inside, admiring it.

Inside the shop, they were surprised to see Flavio standing right inside the door, watching them. It was as though he was expecting them to return. His face was markedly full of suspicion.

Patty held up the painting and said, in Sicilian, that she wanted to purchase it.

Still watching her with narrowed eyes, he took her purchase into the back, laid it on the counter, and started to wrap it. As he did, Audrey whispered to Patty, "Can you ask him if he saw the shooting yesterday?"

She did.

He didn't look up from taping up the craft paper as he shook his head. "No."

"You're lying," Audrey stated.

His head whipped up to hers.

Audrey began, "Tell him—"

"Of course I'm lying!" he shouted in perfect English. "You stupid Americans don't know what it's like to live in a town ruled by the mob! People who stick their necks out get their heads cut off! *Stupido!*"

Her eyes widened. She looked at Patty, who seemed just as surprised. Patty held out her hand. "Hello. I'm Patty Randazzo. I'm a Piccolo."

His face went a sick white. He swallowed, finished taping up her purchase, and pushed it over to her. "No charge."

She shook her head and pulled out her wallet, laying a few euros down on the counter. "Oh, please. That's not what I wanted. I'm telling you this because the man who was killed was my boyfriend, Bruno, and I really loved him, and want to know what happened to him."

The man's lips twisted. He closed his eyes and let out a sigh. "Fine. I did not see much. But I do know it was a man who shot. I found the shells in my backyard, so he must've been behind the fence. I saw someone running, a few moments after the shooting. A hunter. He had a large gun."

Audrey's eyes bulged. "Do you know where we can find this man . . . what's his name?"

"Franco Testo. He lives outside of town, in the Monti Sicani, in the cabin near the old *frazione.*"

Patty said, "*Ficuzza?*"

He nodded. "That's right."

"What's that?" Audrey asked, confused.

"It's a hamlet in the mountains where hunters used to live." She frowned. "It's about ten miles away. I know where it is."

Audrey gnawed on her lip, then nodded. "All right. I think we need to go and check it out."

CHAPTER TWENTY ONE

When they returned to the convertible, Patty lugging the painting she'd bought, Audrey had a new fire lit under her. The clock was still ticking, and the trip out to the unknown would take precious time. But this was the first solid lead they had. The first true bit of news that established there was someone else besides Marco Capaldi behind the gun.

"Oh, dang it," Patty said as she pointed out the road to take. "I forgot to check at the café to see if they had any more of those yummy pastries."

"How can you think about food at a time like this?"

"I might not be thinking about it, but my tum-tum is," she said, patting her flat stomach. "You can probably hear it growling. Sounds like the creature from the black lagoon."

"Yeah, but we're finally getting somewhere."

She made a face. "If it's not someplace with pastries, I'm not interested."

"But don't you see what this means?" Audrey said as she followed Patty's pointed finger out of town. "This proves someone other than Marco Capaldi did it."

"Whoopie," she said, less than enthusiastically. "I thought we confirmed that before."

"No. I mean, *I* thought the same, but your uncle Carmine passed it off as the Capaldis paying people off to keep quiet about Marco's whereabouts. Flavio had nothing to gain by telling us what he saw, and everything to lose. So it's something your uncle can't ignore."

"Carmine's a tough nut. You really think he's going to take the word of crazy old junk man?"

Audrey shook her head. "Rafael said the only thing that would stop his father from ordering that hit was if someone else was arrested for the crime. That's why we're going to check into this Franco Testo. If he's a good enough lead, we'll tell the police. And if they question him and arrest him, then the case is closed. Right?"

"Right," she said doubtfully. "I guess you're right. We are getting somewhere. Only, I don't quite understand why this random hunter would want my Bruno dead."

"That's what we're going to find out."

"Maybe the Capaldis paid him to . . . no, that doesn't make sense. No self-respecting family would farm out their hits to someone who isn't a brother. Right?"

Audrey looked at her and shrugged. "You would know better than I do."

Patty drummed her long fingernails on the armrest. "Bruno said that as an outsider, he had to go through a long initiation to be considered one of them. Even though Luigi and I have known him forever. They vet their people like crazy. I can't see them hiring someone outside of their circle to make the hit." She gnawed on her lip.

"So Bruno never mentioned any enemies, outside of his dealings with the Piccolo family?"

"No! Bruno was a big teddy bear. Everyone liked him. Even the Capaldis liked him. He was a really nice guy." She was quiet for a moment, and then added, "That's why, when he told me Luigi had convinced him to join, I laughed. Obviously, we weren't dating then, but I told him he was out of his mind. I didn't think he had it in him to be a real Piccolo. Like Carmine."

"Or Rafael?"

She shook her head. "Rafael's gentle, too. It takes a certain kind of man to do the ruthless things the Piccolos have been known to do in the past. Sandro? Now, I could see him being don. He's always considered himself better than everyone else. He'd continue things on, just like Carmine. But Rafael? He's always been different. But truthfully, I wouldn't mind it. Everyone is tired of it. Maybe it's time we stop fighting like children."

Audrey pressed on the gas, that thought firmly in her mind. She couldn't help feeling that whatever she found at the end of this ride might affect the fate of the Piccolo family—the fate of the entire town of Corleone—forever. "These hamlets . . ."

"It's just a little village outside of the city, from what I hear." She hooked an arm out the open window. "But I know the cabin. Bruno and I used to go on drives. You can just barely see it from the road. It's not part of the village."

Meaning, it was secluded. If this man, Franco Testo, was the murderer, and things got tense, there'd be no one to save them.

"Patty," she said. "When we go there, we're going to have to use a lot of tact so as not to upset him."

"Me? Upset people?" She batted her eyelashes innocently. "I don't think so."

"Well . . .Bruno's ex-wife . . ." she pointed out, once again.

"But she was a *witch*."

"All right. But just keep in mind that this man has a gun. Let's not give him any reason to use it. Okay?"

She shrugged. "Okay. Fine."

They slowly climbed a steep incline, into mountains covered with golden grass and scrub brush. Tendrils of Patty's hair, which had been piled on top of her head in something like a beehive hairdo of old, were now loose, flapping in the breeze. She pushed them out of her eyes. "It's somewhere around here, I'm sure." She jumped up. "There it is! In here! Turn here!"

Audrey hung a quick right into a dirt driveway, then paused at the sign posted on a single tree at the entrance of the drive: *Attenzione pericolo di morte.*

Her nose wrinkled. "What does that mean?"

"It means there's grave danger if you pass," Patty said with a bit too much nonchalance. She shrugged. "Sicilians are very dramatic. Why put up a simple *No trespassing* sign when you can scare the living daylights out of someone?"

"Oh." Well, it definitely did the trick. Audrey looked around, her skin prickling with goosebumps. "Should we—"

"Drive. We want to know what this guy has to say for himself, right?"

Audrey nodded. It was the only way.

They took a long, winding path to a small, stone cottage that had once been painted red. The crumbling stone wall and an old, rotting pickup truck had practically been swallowed up by long, yellow grass.

"Does anyone live here?" Audrey asked as they approached. "It looks deserted."

Patty shrugged as Audrey cut the engine and they climbed out of the car.

The moment Audrey looked up, she saw a curtain in the window fall back into place. "Someone's in there."

She went to the door, which was just three wide planks of decaying wood tacked together. As she was about to knock, she noticed some animal pelts draped over the porch railing. Not rabbits, but . . .

"Ew. Squirrels," Patty said aloud, completing her thought. "You think he eats them? Ew. I want to barf."

Audrey shrugged and knocked.

The man who answered was tall and thin, with a long, drawn face, his chin dotted with white stubble. His dark eyes were so sunken in his face that he reminded Audrey of a skeleton. It made a chill flitter down her spine. *"Ciao. Franco Testo?"*

He regarded her warily. *"Si."* He pointed forcefully at the road and said something that Audrey was able to translate to, *Didn't you see the sign?*

Audrey nodded. "Yes, but I wonder if I might ask you a few questions. Can I speak with you? Do you speak English?"

He frowned and looked at Patty, who said in Sicilian, "Or would you rather speak in Sicilian?"

He let out a defeated sigh. His voice was a low rumble as he said in English, "What is this about?"

"I'm sure you heard about the shooting in town yesterday," Audrey said.

He shook his head. "I don't pay much mind to anything going on in town. That is why I live out here. To get away from that."

He's lying.

That, Audrey knew instantly. She looked down, trying to formulate her next question as delicately as possible. The first thing she noticed was that the man had massive feet—he was barefoot, and his toes looked like long, dirty hooks. The second thing she noticed was the hunting rifle, propped up right beside the door Easy to pick up at a moment's notice, say, to shoot at intruders?

Oh, no.

Before she could back away, Patty said, "I think you're lying. You're a lying liar who lies!"

Audrey glanced at her, trying to warn her to stop, but Patty simply shrugged. "What? It's written all over his face!"

The man scowled at her, and his hand moved ever so slightly toward his weapon. Audrey plastered her sweetest smile on her face. "Well, you see, we just came from town and we heard that somebody spotted you there. So we thought maybe you could give us some insight into the case? Tell us what you saw?"

He didn't flinch. "That somebody's wrong. I was not there."

"They also found shell casings in the backyard of the antiques shop, belonging to a rifle. Do you know anything about that?"

He shook his head. "Plenty of other hunters in this area besides me."

"Yeah, but you were the one spotted there," Patty pointed out. "No way to mistake this tall, skinny guy for someone else. The shopkeeper would have to be blind to do that."

Audrey had to agree, though she wished her companion would be a little more tactful. She motioned to the gun, but Patty seemed oblivious. "Hmm?" she continued. "What do you have to say about that?"

For a moment, he didn't speak at all. He didn't move. Audrey held her breath. Then he simply went to close the door. "Get off my property."

Fine. Good idea. They'd go back to town, tell the police officers what they'd learned, and go on their merry way, letting the police take it from there. They'd done all they could.

Audrey took another step back in retreat, but suddenly, Patty put a foot forward into the door, impressively holding it open with just her kitten heel. "What do you think you're doing? We're not done with you!"

His eyes narrowed. Audrey reached for her arm. "Actually, Patty, we kind of are!"

"No! No, I'm not leaving here until I get some answers!" she shouted, shoving the door with her full weight to keep it open. "You killed my boyfriend, you big, skinny jerk!"

She pushed in and began to pummel his chest. For a moment, he just stood there, nonplussed, hardly affected by the jabs of this tiny, five-foot-two woman. Then, with little effort, he reached down and scooped the rifle into his hands.

She backed up at once, hands up in surrender, her mouth in the shape of an O. "Whoa, you don't have to overreact . . ."

Talk about overreacting, Audrey thought, stumbling back off the porch, onto the grass.

"Get. Off. My. Property. NOW!"

Audrey grabbed hold of the sleeve of Patty's kimono and tugged her. This time, she relented, scuffing to the car. When she was there, she gave him the finger and called, "You haven't heard the last of us!"

He cocked the rifle and leaned in, aiming it right at her.

Audrey flinched. Patty didn't. She seemed to pay no mind to the barrel of the gun pointed straight at her. "Scumbag!"

"Get in the car," she said under her breath, willing her heart to start beating again. She tried to ignore the gun, but in the heightened tension, her pulse roaring, her hands shaking, it was all she could see. *"Please!"*

But Patty stood outside the door of the car, taunting him with what were probably Sicilian insults, adding more rude gestures. Audrey reached across the passenger side and shoved on the door, bumping Patty's hip, but it did no good.

"Patty!" Audrey said louder, seeing the whole scene so clearly in her mind. The gun going off. Patty slumping to the ground, mid-insult. The blood. Patty, staring up at the sky before she passed into oblivion, murmuring, *Why, Awd? Why didn't you tell me?* Shouting, now: "Patty!"

Finally, Patty whirled and looked at her. "What?"

Audrey opened her mouth to tell her to get in the car when she heard the sound of tires crunching over gravel, coming from behind her. In the rearview mirror, she saw a cloud of dust in the driveway.

A few minutes later, a police car emerged from the haze.

Audrey sighed in relief. But that was short-lived, because Patty suddenly shouted, "Stop him! He's getting away!"

Sure enough, the man dashed to the edge of the porch, still carrying his rifle and preparing to dive into the bushes at the edge of the house. As he did, Patty threw off her kitten heels and broke into a run. Audrey tried to scramble from the car, but by the time she got out, he'd made the leap. He climbed from the tangle of branches just as Patty reached him.

"Don't you go anywhere!" she shouted at him, grabbing his arm.

It was a classic David and Goliath play, but unfortunately, Goliath won out. He wrapped an arm around her waist and pulled her to his chest, just as the police emerged from the car, guns drawn, shouting, *"Fermi! Fermi! Giù le armi!"*

The man sneered at them and shook his head wildly. "No! Never."

In shock, Audrey watched the standoff from the open driver's side door. "I think he's the shooter," she said to the officers. "The shopkeeper saw him in the area right after the shooting."

The older one nodded tensely, never taking his eyes off the man who'd taken Patty hostage. "We spoke to the shopkeeper and asked him what he told you, then we followed you here."

Patty sighed and shifted under the man's grip. "Would you let go of me! You *smell*!" she groused, then called to the officers, "Shoot him, already!"

124

The officers moved forward. Franco took a step backwards, toward the back of his yard. Clenching his rifle at his side, he glanced behind him. Beyond the edge of his house was miles and miles of barren wilderness, scrubby bushes, and grass that rose into the desolate, rock-covered hills.

Then he raised his rifle and pointed it at the officers. Already cocked, he only needed one hand to pull the trigger.

Audrey held her breath, waiting for the inevitable gunshot.

Instead, Patty wrenched herself free, elbowed the rifle from his grip, then wheeled around and kicked him, barefoot, square in the family jewels.

"Take that, you *fiend*," she shouted at him as he doubled over, moaning in pain. "That'll teach you never to lay a hand on me!"

She stepped away from him, fixing her hair into place.

Audrey could only stare as the officers advanced. The older one lifted the man up and snapped cuffs on him.

Patty ran to the younger one as he shoved his gun back into his holster. She jumped into his arms. "My hero!" she said, planting a kiss on his cheek.

He grinned. "That was some kick."

Franco Testo moaned as the older officer guided him toward the police car. "I didn't do it! I didn't kill that man."

"Right!" Patty called out. "Tell that to the judge!"

"You were spotted at the scene," the older officer said, opening the back door for him.

"No," he shouted, "you don't understand. Yes, I was there. I was poaching squirrels from the yard. That was all. But I did not shoot any man. I promise you that! I am no murder—"

His voice was cut off by the slamming of the car door.

Audrey looked at Patty, who was now in a lip-lock with the young officer. "Um . . . Bruno?" she said, snapping her fingers at the woman.

Patty shrugged, red-faced. "Bruno would want me to be happy."

The officer's eyes widened. "Wait. You and the shooting victim were . . ." He swallowed. "Are you saying you're . . ."

"A Piccolo?" She nodded.

He stepped away immediately and pulled on the collar of his uniform. "I've got to go," he said, rushing so quickly back to the police car, he was practically a blur.

Patty sighed. "Oh, well. The life of a mafia princess. Easy come, easy go."

Audrey checked her phone and slipped behind the wheel of the convertible. "Come on. We have to get back to Cielo d'Azzurro. Your uncle is about to order that hit, and hopefully, this news will be enough to stop him."

CHAPTER TWENTY TWO

As they made their way back to the Piccolo estate, Patty was unusually quiet. "What's wrong?" Audrey asked her. "Are you okay?"

"I was just thinking about my life."

Audrey gave her a sideways glance. "That's pretty deep. What about your life?"

"Well, my mother is Carmine's great-great-aunt's granddaughter. Or something. I forget. There's some relation there. My mom was brought up in the family, but decided to move to the United States to escape the mafia. She married Paul Randazzo and lived in Newark. We had a pizza place downtown. A quiet life. My mom never talked about her family. I didn't know about the whole mafia thing until I was eight years old and started asking about them. That was when we took our first trip out here, and I've come every year since." She shrugged. "I sometimes wonder what my life would've been like if I hadn't asked about my family. Who I would be. I wouldn't be Patty the mafia girl. I'd be a different person. Maybe Bruno wouldn't be dead. Maybe Leo and I would have a chance."

"Leo?"

"That police officer." She frowned. "Curiosity killed the cat. I should've left well enough alone and not asked my mother about her family."

"Yes . . . but good things came from it, too, right?"

She shrugged. "I guess. Not much." She shook her head. "The thing is, with all those DNA kits available online, people are so interested in knowing about their past, but what is that going to do? You have no control over it. Better to focus on the present. You can do something about that. Right?"

Audrey nodded. "Right. But you did it. And you found your family here in Sicily. I don't think you should feel bad about it. After all, what's done is done. Right?"

"Yeah." She dropped her chin to her chest and sniffled a little.

In the ensuing silence, Audrey thought about her father. She knew there was no mafia in Miles Smart's history, but he was her father, and that meant that she'd spent every day wondering what he'd done. Why he'd left. Whatever the reason, it probably wasn't anything good. He'd left because he wanted to, and he hadn't sought her out again. Maybe finding him would open up secrets and wounds that would hurt her more. Maybe that part of her past deserved to stay buried. After all, she had a pretty good life; maybe she should just focus on the now, instead.

"Oh. My. *Gawd!*" Patty shouted suddenly. "I can't believe that whole thing just happened. That was pretty wild."

"I can't believe you kicked that guy in the crotch," Audrey said with a laugh. "That took guts!"

Patty pushed her hair back into place, but with the breeze blowing through the convertible, it came right out again. "Why, Audrey, you act as though you've never been held in a standoff before."

"I haven't. God forbid," Audrey laughed, then looked at Patty, who seemed entirely serious. "Wait. You have?"

She nodded. "Twice. Oh, but only in the first one was I in actual danger. Some drug deal gone bad. Wrong place, wrong time. The second was nothing. Just a little drunken misunderstanding between family. Luigi thought Bruno was disrespecting me, and he didn't like it. Almost shot Bruno's head off. That's where I learned that little elbow move. Pretty good, huh?"

Audrey nodded. "That's . . . impressive."

"Like I said, ever since I found out about my family on the other side of the world, my life has been very different," she said with a sigh. "So are you going to talk to Uncle Carmine when we get back to the house?"

"Yeah. I only hope this is enough to dissuade him from continuing with that hit on Marco Capaldi," she said, drumming her fingers on the steering wheel. "What I don't understand, though, is why Franco Testo would do that. What was his motive?"

Patty shrugged.

"You don't think the Capaldis would have hired him, right, to do the hit?" Audrey asked.

"No. Definitely not. They only trust their own network. And that scruffy guy? He doesn't look anything like one of them." She shook her head. "Nope. He's a lone wolf."

"Okay, then . . ."

"Maybe it was an accident?" Patty ventured. "You heard him. He was shooting squirrels. Maybe one of his bullets went haywire."

"That wasn't an accidental shooting. And it was *two* bullets. Plus, if he was killing animals in the yard, how would he miss and shoot someone all the way on the other side of the street? I'm no gun expert, but it sounds fishy, doesn't it?"

Patty nodded. "Yeah. You're right."

They pulled down the driveway to the Piccolo villa as the sun was starting to slip below the mountains. It was 6:45. Audrey sighed and said, "Well, fingers crossed your uncle buys it and doesn't decide to go through with this craziness."

As Audrey went inside, she shivered. Carmine was bloodthirsty, just looking for a reason to start that war with the Capaldis. Maybe he wouldn't listen to her. Maybe he'd order the hit anyway.

Once again, when they went inside, the place was quiet. Audrey walked toward the office and paused at the door, listening. Hearing nothing, she whispered to Patty, "What if they already left? What if—"

She stopped when Rafael came down the stairs, followed by Rocco and Sandro. All three were wearing suits, and looked as though they were ready to go out. Rafael's face was grim. He raised an eyebrow when he saw her. "Audrey. You're back."

"Oh, thank goodness you're here. I thought you already left," she said, her words coming out in a tumble. "Where is your father?"

He motioned to the door, then rapped once. A voice told them to come in. Rafael looked at her. "Did you find something? Why do you look out of breath?"

"They arrested someone for Bruno's murder!" Patty said loudly.

Rafael's eyes widened and shifted between them. "It's true? Who?"

Audrey opened her mouth to speak, but he put up a finger and opened the door. Carmine was standing behind his desk, and as she'd noticed during dinner the night before, he was shorter than she would have expected.

"Father," Rafael said, beckoning Audrey in. "Audrey brings news from town. Apparently, there has been an arrest in Bruno's murder."

He stiffened. "An arrest?"

Audrey nodded. "His name is—"

"Franco Testo," Patty spoke up from behind her. "He's this gross hunting dude with huge feet."

Audrey nodded, then turned to Carmine, anxiously awaiting his reaction. "Franco . . ." he murmured, deep in thought. "How was this determined?"

"The shopkeeper at the antiques store in town saw him leaving the scene of the crime. He had a gun with him. He was hiding behind the

129

fence. He says he was just shooting squirrels, but apparently that's not all he was shooting at."

Carmine nodded. "I see."

Audrey cleared her throat and said, "We still don't know what possible motive he could have had, but maybe the police will—"

"I do."

Audrey froze. "You do?"

Carmine nodded. "He'd been poaching squirrels on our land. I didn't like it. I told him he would get one of us shot, so I told him he needed to find another place. He threatened me. He was bitter."

Audrey's mouth opened slightly. "Oh." Her nose wrinkled. "And he shot your men because of . . . squirrels? That seems a little . . . excessive."

Patty shrugged. "He was off his rocker, *Awd*. You saw him." She twirled a finger by her ear. "Crazy."

"I guess," she said, turning back to the don. She hoped he'd say something. Applaud her. Give her another Piccolo coin. Something. Anything that would ease her mind and tell her that he was no longer going through with this terrible hit.

But he simply nodded. "*Grazie*," he said, and pointed to the door.

"But—" she asked, but didn't complete her sentence because at that moment, she caught sight of Rafael. His eyes warned, *Do as he says.*

Carmine said, "I must speak with my men. Please leave."

She didn't argue this time. She went to the door, casting one last glance at Rafael and his men as she closed the door. Rafael looked stiff and uncomfortable. Next to him, Alessandro winked at her.

Outside, she said to Patty, "I don't think that went so well."

Patty went to the door and put her ear up to it. "Shoot. I can't hear anything. Ten to one, Sandro convinces them to go for it anyway. He's just as happy to start this war as Carmine is."

Audrey went to the stairs and sat down on the second-to-bottom one, then put her head in her hands. "I don't understand it. Why would they want to? There's nothing to prove. It's not mob related at all. Why would they want to risk more people getting killed?"

"Because they're macho men, with their guns. They like to show off." Patty hugged herself and kicked at the bottom step. "I know, it's stupid. Sometimes I really wish I wasn't a Piccolo."

Just then, the door flew open and Rafael came out. "Audrey!"

She stood up. "Yes."

He went over to her and took her hands. His normally smooth, unemotional voice was full of excitement. "My father decided that the arrest was enough to put this to bed. He decided not to go ahead with the hit."

"Really?"

He nodded, and suddenly he pulled her in for a tight hug. He pulled away just long enough to kiss her, not exactly on the cheek, but not on the lips either—in that little space between. "Thank you," he whispered into her ear. "This was all your doing, and I'm grateful. If there is anything I can do for you . . ."

She smiled. "Well, I already have the Piccolo coin."

He straightened and looked at her, still holding both of her hands in his own. "Yes. But I'm going to put extra attention on finding your father, Miles Smart. I'll go to the ends of the Earth for that. For you."

She glanced at Patty, remembering her words: *People are so interested in knowing about their past, but what is that going to do? You have no control over it. Better to focus on the present. You can do something about that.* "You know what? Maybe it's better that he's not found."

He raised an eyebrow. "Are you sure?"

She nodded. "I think I'm dealing with enough, just finding myself first."

"All right," he said, leaning forward again. This time, she thought he might hit the mark, but instead, he kissed her forehead, right above the hairline, and then walked away.

And strangely, she realized she was okay with it. Like she'd said, she had enough on her hands, just finding herself. Plus, she had Mason, and G, and everything else, waiting for her back in Mussomeli. Which reminded her . . .

She whirled. "Rafael!"

He turned. "Yes?"

"Does this mean we're going back to Mussomeli tonight? I have the clinic to go back to tomorrow, and—"

"Of course." He smiled at her. "I can at least do that for you. But what do you say we have some more of my father's amazing pasta before we head back? It's already on the stove."

She smiled, and her mouth began to water as she realized she hadn't had anything to eat all day. "Absolutely. I can't wait."

CHAPTER TWENTY THREE

Audrey should have felt relieved as she changed into a bright yellow sundress and got ready for her last dinner at the Piccolo estate. The place, once quiet and morose, was now in a bit of a celebratory mood. Soft music wafted in from the open windows, and she could hear people laughing outside. She fluffed her long hair, applied lip gloss, and slipped on some dangly earrings, then admired her reflection in the mirror.

Not bad, she thought to herself. *If Rafael is ever going to make a move on you, it'll be tonight.*

She realized her teeth were clenched, and pulled them apart. Something was wrong. Part of it was that she wasn't sure about Rafael. Patty Randazzo's life was clearly difficult because of her mafia connections. Did Audrey want that kind of complication in her life? Did she like Rafael so much that it didn't matter?

She wasn't sure. The truth was, he didn't make her heart beat like crazy. And so that meant . . . no. That meant that if he did try something, she'd have to let him down easy.

If that was even possible. He may have been a kinder, gentler Piccolo, but he was still a Piccolo.

But as she swept a mascara wand over her eyelashes, she realized that wasn't all.

Something else was bothering her.

Something about . . . Franco Testo.

She shook it off. *Oh, stop it, Audrey. You're not thinking straight because you're starving. Franco was clearly the killer. He was crazy, like Patty said. And upset that Carmine had taken his favorite hunting spot from him.*

As she walked to the door, she nearly jumped when she saw a dark form in the window.

She whirled, only to see Nick. He jumped on the vanity and hopped his way over to the bed. "There you are!" she called to him. "I was wondering about you, Bub. I hope you haven't been getting into as much trouble as I've been."

He sat up straight, licking his paws.

She reached over to pet him. "Ready to go home tonight? Now, I don't want you going far, so make sure you stay close. I don't want to be running around at night looking for you."

He licked her hand.

"Oh, you're hungry." She thought about Carmine's distaste for animals and said, "It's probably best if you don't come in here right now. The don doesn't go around shooting squirrels with a rifle, but he doesn't really like little animals too much. Go outside and wait in the garden. We're eating out there in a little bit. I'm sure someone will drop some food for you. If they don't, I will."

He seemed to nod, then turned about, his fuzzy tail tickling her arm as he went. He jumped back onto the vanity and headed out the window, disappearing behind the frame.

As she opened the door to the bedroom, she imagined the powerful don, Carmine, hiding behind a fence, picking off defenseless squirrels with his big rifle. The image brought a smile to her face. Men like Carmine didn't carry big guns like that. They were much more sophisticated. They preferred pistols, something they could slide in a shoulder holster, undetected.

Suddenly, something occurred to her.

By the time she made it to the foot of the stairs, the seed that had been planted in her head had grown, and now she couldn't get it out, even if she wanted to. The more she thought about it, the more confused she became.

She needed to talk it out with someone.

Patty. Patty will tell me if I'm just being crazy.

But Patty hadn't been in their room while she was getting ready. In the foyer, she looked around the house, wondering where she might be.

It didn't take long to think of just the place.

As she turned to head out to the pool, she ran across Luigi. He was standing in the hallway, where the walls were adorned with photographs. Audrey hadn't paid much attention to them, because most of them were photographs of Carmine, with various associates she didn't know. But Luigi was staring at one photograph in particular, his brow wrinkled, his mouth slightly open, as if he was trying to commit it to memory, so he didn't even notice her when she approached.

"Hey, Luigi. Good to see you up. How is your arm?"

He blinked out of the trance he was in and said, "Good. *Grazie.*"

"I was looking for Patty. Did you happen to see her?" she asked, her eyes trailing to the photograph.

It was one of three children—two boys and a girl. They couldn't have been more than ten or eleven. The girl was unabashedly wearing a hot pink bikini, and had her arm around both boys as they stood at the seashore.

Luigi nodded. "She went out to the pool," he said, his eyes turning back to the picture.

Suddenly, Audrey understood. "That's you three, isn't it? Patty, Bruno, and you. Right?"

He nodded. "It was the first time I met her. She came here to spend the summer, and the three of us got along . . . very well." He coughed. For a moment, Audrey thought he might be choking back tears. "We were like brothers, the two of us. We fought a lot, but we were close. And then she came along. And then it was always just the three of us . . ."

She squinted at the photograph. There was a caption that said, *Bruno Mercucci, Patricia Randazzo, Luigi Fiore . . . San Vito Lo Capo, 2000.*

"Oh, I'm sorry. I know you must miss him very much."

"*Si,*" he said, his voice far away. "I do."

She went past him. "Well, something smells good. You'll be there for dinner?"

He nodded.

"Good. See you then."

When she went outside, servants were there, setting up a long table for all the close family members underneath the covered patio. The display was something out of a magazine spread, and the food smelled delicious. Audrey sneaked a hand into the salad and stole a cherry tomato. Popping it into her mouth, she took the stairs to the pool.

Sure enough, Patty was there, completely submerged except for her pile of hair, which was dry, a pair of sunglasses hopelessly lost within it. She was doggy-paddling through the water, smiling. "I finally made it in! And look—no Sandro in sight!" she called to Audrey. "Where's your suit? You should come in, too."

"I didn't bring one." The sun had now almost completely set, but there were lights on around the pool and underneath the water. "Looks like dinner will be ready soon anyway."

Patty sighed. "I guess I should get out and towel off. Don't want to be eating in a wet bathing suit."

Audrey crouched at the side of the pool as Patty paddled toward the ladder. "Hey. I was thinking about something. About Franco Testo."

She pulled herself up, climbed the ladder, and grabbed her towel, patting herself dry. "What about him?"

"Well, I was thinking about the bullet. Luigi showed me the bullet that had been taken from his shoulder. It was a tiny one, like, smaller than a dime. Correct me if I'm wrong, but I didn't think those kinds of bullets came from rifles."

Patty nodded as she sat down on the lounge chair to dry her legs. "Yeah. They don't." Her brow wrinkled. "Weird. But maybe what Luigi showed you was just a fragment of a bullet?"

"I don't think so. It looked like a regular bullet, just misshapen. Very small."

"Hmm." Patty wrapped the towel around her mid-section. "There has to be some reasonable explanation. Maybe he used a different gun. Franco's clearly the killer."

Audrey eyed the Jersey girl, doubtful. "I don't know. Is he?"

"Oh, don't doubt yourself, girl. I can't tell you how glad I was that they arrested someone. It was such a weight off my shoulders. The funeral's on Wednesday. I'll so happy to be able to put all this behind us. For good."

Audrey nodded. "You're right." She pointed toward the garden. "I'm going to take a little walk before dinner."

She wandered into the gardens, inhaling the flower-scented air and listening to the insects buzzing about. She tried to let the relief wash over her. And yet something kept tugging at her. It would be so easy to simply say "case closed" and move on with their lives. It seemed like everyone in the house wanted to do just that. But Audrey couldn't.

She sat down on a bench, found a stick, and started drawing out the scene of the crime. The corner where the murder had occurred, the antiques store, with its fence and many bushes, the café, and the road. She stared at it until it was etched in her mind, even when she closed her eyes.

"There you are," a voice said.

She looked up to find Rafael, walking toward her in the semi-darkness.

"It's getting too dark out here and we don't have any lights in the garden. You should come in. Dinner is almost served, anyway."

She smiled. "Are there wild animals out here that'll eat me?"

"I think that fox of yours will protect you." He chuckled.

She had to agree. Nick had helped her out of plenty of rough spots. "It's a very nice night."

"It is, but . . ." His eyes hitched on the map she'd drawn in the dirt. "What have you been up to?"

"I was just thinking . . ." she admitted. "What errand were the two boys on again? It was one for Carmine, right?"

"Yes. Like I said, nothing illegal. They went to a Signore Filardo's house to deliver a check to someone. He lives on the other side of the antiques shop."

"A check . . . for what?"

"Well, it's a funny thing. The boys were out driving and hit Filardo's car that was parked on the street. So Filardo contacted Carmine, and he agreed to pay for the damages."

"They hit a parked car? How do you do that?"

He shrugged and laughed. "Right? It was in broad daylight, on a straightaway, too. I guess you'd have to ask Luigi that one."

She pointed to the diagram. "How far away was the antiques shop from that corner where Bruno was shot?"

He frowned. "I thought we were all done with this."

"I know, I know," she said, exasperated. "But can you humor me? Please?"

He sat down next to her and rubbed his chin. "Pretty far. I'd say a thousand meters."

"And what's the maximum distance you think a gun can shoot?"

He shrugged. "It depends on the gun. And the person. Some sharpshooters can hit a target thousands of meters away."

"But the average guy?"

He raised his palms up. "I don't know. Probably a thousand meters, at most."

"Right. And there was that solid fence, and all those bushes, and . . ."

He studied her. "What are you saying?"

She laughed sadly. "I don't know what I'm saying. Maybe I am going crazy. I always get this way. I can't stop wondering if I put the wrong guy in jail."

He reached over and massaged her shoulder. "You didn't. You did well. Our family is grateful for everything you've done."

"Your father won't . . . um, arrange a hit for this guy? This Franco? While he's in jail? As payback for killing Bruno?"

"Ah, you are so worried about that? Gentle girl. No. You need not worry. He'll let the justice system work this through," he said. "Please. Enjoy the meal tonight. Then we will go back to Mussomeli and you can concentrate on your practice and your home. Everything will work out, I promise you."

She nodded, just as the horn to summon the wild animals sounded, coming from the direction of the house.

"Ah," he said, standing and offering her his arm. "Dinner is ready. What do you say we go in and have some of my father's pasta?"

*

They dined by candlelight on the covered patio. It was twelve of them—Audrey, Patty, Rafael, Luigi, Rocco, Franco, Leo, Sandro, and several other members of the family who Audrey had been briefly introduced to, but whose names she now forgot.

Carmine wasn't there. Word was that he was too busy. It seemed that he missed out on a lot of the family dinners. As usual, it was rowdy and lively, with lots of laughter. Audrey got the feeling it would be a lot more subdued if the don *had* been there. But now, the wine was flowing, spirits were high, and everyone seemed to be in a good mood.

This time, it was vodka rigatoni, fresh warm bread, as well as a fresh caprese salad with cherry tomatoes, mozzarella, and balsamic glaze. The meal had always been one of Audrey's favorites, even in the States, so after second glass of wine, she found herself relaxing and forgetting about the past day's events. They were all reminiscing, and even though Audrey hadn't been a part of their memories, she couldn't help but laugh about some of their crazy adventures.

Rafael told a story about a big reunion they'd had when most of them were just teenagers. "Whose idea was it to take that donkey ride into the hills? What a nightmare that was."

Patty, across from her, laughed and nudged Luigi. "That was yours, Luigi."

Luigi simply looked at her and shrugged.

Sandro said, "I think I remember that."

Patty shook her head. "You can't have. You were barely a toddler! But I remember it. I refused to take the reins and ride my own so I wound up riding with Bruno? Remember, Luigi, how you fought like cats and dogs over who got stuck with me?"

Luigi tossed back the rest of his wine and stared into the glass. "No, I don't."

Rafael laughed. "Those two, fighting? Who would've thought?"

137

Everyone roared with laughter, except Luigi, who seemed to shrink into his chair at the incessant ribbing. It was nice to see them happily reminiscing about their time with Bruno.

Patty nudged him again. "Oh, come on, Luigi. You know you two have been going at it forever. Geez. Ever since I've known you two, you've been at each other's throats over absolutely nothing!"

He looked over at her, but did not speak.

There was something in his expression that struck Audrey. Everyone else was enjoying themselves, but he seemed to be lost in thought, his movements stiff and annoyed. Finally, as the ribbing continued, he said, "Enough."

Then he pushed away from the table, stood up, threw his napkin on the table, and stalked away, heading down the stairs and into the gardens.

Sandro laughed. "Looks like someone doesn't know how to take a joke, huh?"

"Oh," Patty glowered at him. "Stop. He's obviously still hurt about poor Bruno. They were so close."

As Audrey watched Luigi run off, she sighed in sympathy for him. Watching him see his best friend killed in cold blood had probably been too much for him. He couldn't joke about it now. The wounds were probably still as fresh as his physical injury.

Or was he upset for another reason?

Suddenly, something struck her. She stared after him, thinking of the way he'd looked at that photograph. *Luigi Fiore.*

Fiore.

Her eyes went to the flowered centerpiece. *Fiori.* That's what Bruno had been trying to communicate to her, just before he died, his eyes wild with fear. She'd thought he'd been speaking of the flowers in the centerpiece.

But that was silly. Why would he be speaking of those? Maybe, just maybe, he'd been trying to tell her something else.

Maybe he'd been trying to tell her the name of his killer.

In an instant, her blood ran cold. Rafael was in the middle of telling her something, but she barely heard the words. She slipped her own napkin off her lap and stood up.

"Everything okay?" Rafael asked, looking up at her. "We still have tiramisu for dessert."

She nodded. "I'll be back. I just need to . . ." She pointed.

He must've thought she was going to the restroom, because he turned and once again became absorbed in the conversation. It was easier, then, for her to slip out the steps from the patio and follow the pathway into the gardens.

As she walked, it only became clearer and clear in her mind.

They'd had the wrong man arrested for Bruno's murder.

And now was her chance to make things right.

CHAPTER TWENTY FOUR

The moon was full as she walked along the garden path, providing just enough light for Audrey to see where she was going. She stepped carefully along the smooth gray cobblestones that seemed to glow in the minimal light, trying to make out any sign of Luigi among the dark hedges and flowering bushes around her.

Luigi was gone.

Maybe he found a way back to the house.

The lively music coming from the patio faded off, and replace by the sound of the trickling fountain up ahead. She followed that sound to the clearing, with the small fountain and four benches surrounding the fountain in a circle.

The rippling water reflected the moon brightly, and several coins shone underneath. She wondered if any of them were wishes.

Right then, if she could've wished for anything, she wanted to get away from this danger. She wanted to go home.

Home. Funny, when she thought that word, she didn't think of Boston. She thought of Mussomeli.

Just when she reached the fountain, she looked across the other side of the statue at its center, and saw Luigi, his back to her. He had his good hand in his pocket, and was staring up at the sky.

"Luigi," she called.

Startled, he whipped his head around. When he saw it was only her, he let out an annoyed sigh. "Go away. Can't I be in peace?"

"Is everything all right?" she said carefully, stepping around the fountain, moving closer to him. "You seemed a little rattled back there."

"I'm . . ." He seemed as though he was about to say something, but then he looked down. He pointed to his arm. "I'm fine. Just . . . my painkillers must be wearing off."

She sat down at the edge of the fountain and smiled. "I understand. You see, I have a sister. And I was just thinking about how I'd feel if something happened to her. I know Bruno was like your brother. And so I know it must be terrible for you."

He nodded slightly, but then said, "You have no idea."

"Did you know Bruno's wife?"

"Giada. Yes. I was the best man at their wedding."

"And you liked her?"

He shrugged. "I liked her all right."

"Did you know what kind of marital problems they were having?"

"Yeah. We all did. She wanted him out of the business, and no one leaves this business, once they get in. She didn't understand. She gave him the ultimatum—her or us. He chose us."

"Because he was forced into it?"

"No. Because we're his family. The closest thing to family he'd ever had."

"Did you know that Giada was in a relationship with Marco Capaldi?"

His eyes met hers in the moonlight. He nodded. "Yeah. It was part of the grapevine that she and Marco went to dinner at the Corleone Café every Friday. But she did that—showing off—out of spite for Bruno. By that time, their relationship was dead. Because Bruno had—"

"Bruno and Patty had fallen in love."

He looked down at the ground and nodded. "I guess."

"Two's company, but three's a crowd, right? And you couldn't stand being the odd man out."

His jaw set. His lips curled. "No. That's not it."

"You knew that those two possible scapegoats for Bruno's murder were eating right across the street."

He turned and faced away from her, shaking his head.

"You pulled your gun on Bruno and shot him in the back. But what you didn't expect is that he would turn around and shoot you, too."

"No," he whispered.

"And then you picked him up and put him in the car, and raced him to Cielo d'Azzurro. You knew how badly he was injured. You hoped when you got to Cielo d'Azzurro, he'd be too gravely injured to talk, and counted on the fact that once he got there, it'd be too late to save him. And it was. But only because I treated the wrong person first."

He shrugged, but he did not deny it. Normally, she'd have been afraid, laying all this out to a known mafia hitman. But he was injured. In pain. The Piccolo family and Rafael were just on the other side of the hedge, within shouting distance. And she had the Piccolo coin.

She shook her head and laughed a little to herself. "Stupid me, I thought you and Bruno were both victims. But he alone is the victim. You're the killer."

He whirled and looked at her, still clutching at his injured arm. "No. I am not."

That was a lie. She could read it on his face. All at once, she knew the truth. "Of course. You did. You killed him. You couldn't take him and Patty being together, leaving you alone. You missed his friendship, and you didn't want to lose it. You two argued all the time about it, and it became too much—"

"No. I'm not going to listen to—"

He started to walk away, but she grabbed hold of his arm, which was in a sling. She pulled him around. "You need to listen. If you're the one who did this and an innocent man went to—"

He let out a yelp of pain and doubled over. She quickly let go. Had she hurt him that badly?

But when he straightened, he was holding a pistol in his good hand . . . and it was pointed directly at her.

CHAPTER TWENTY FIVE

Audrey stared down the barrel of the gun, hands raised in surrender.

Luigi might have been injured, but something told her that he was a crack shot. That he would be able to shoot her easily, even more easily than he'd shot his best friend. He was mafia, a cold-blooded killer, through and through.

She glanced around her, hoping against hope that Nick was there and could sink his teeth into Luigi's ankle and distract him so she could run off. He'd been her savior before, countless times. But he was nowhere to be found now. She was alone.

In the silence, she could hear her own heartbeat, the fountain's trickling, and just beyond that, the sound of the music and laughter from the patio. She whispered, "If you shoot me, your family will hear."

"And? I'll just make up a story. You were crazy. You jumped out of nowhere. I thought you were an intruder. It was dark, and I shot." He smiled an unnaturally wide smile. "Don't think it'll work? It already did. Besides, they're my *family*. They'd back me up. You're no one."

"Rafael would never forgive you," she said, though she wasn't sure if it was true.

He snickered. "You really think Rafael cares about you? Don't be stupid. He doesn't care about any woman. We all know you're just his ruse to keep his dad happy. He's just using you, and you fell for it."

She frowned. There was much to process in that statement, but as she stared into the dark barrel of the gun, she couldn't even begin to. "You murdered Bruno. Everyone said you were so close. How could you do that to your best friend? Your brother?"

He snorted. "Some best friend. We were competitors. Always. In everything. From the minute he showed up in my life. I mistakenly took pity on him because he was poor and had no family of his own. I invited him into my family, and he took advantage. He always won. He got the grades. The awards. The girls. Everything. He showed me up all the time. If I expressed interest in it, he wanted it for himself, no matter what it was." He swallowed with difficulty. "On the football team? I

143

was supposed to start. He took my spot. Giada? She was *my* girlfriend first. It was exhausting, I tell you. *Exhausting.*"

"But Patty loved him."

He let out a disgusted growl. "She loved *me* first."

"But you're both part of the same family. Isn't she your cousin?"

"No. Not by blood. The first time I met her, when I was eleven, I was in love," he said, and his voice was lighter and breathier with the memory. "I told Bruno that I was going to marry her one day. Of course, she didn't want anything to do with me romantically, but I didn't care. Every time I saw her, I asked her to marry me. She always said no. She didn't want anything to do with me. But I kept telling her, one day, she'd say yes. And then one day, a couple months ago, I come to find out . . ."

"She and Bruno were together."

He nodded, making a face like he'd tasted something bad. "Yeah. At first, they tried to hide it from me. But then I found out. And I told him, how could he do that to me! We were brothers. And he *knew*. He knew I'd been in love with Patty since the day I met her. Nearly two decades I bled for that woman. And what did he do? He stepped all over me. At that moment . . . I decided. I decided he was no longer my brother and I'd do everything possible to get him out of the Piccolo family. But once you're in . . . there's only one way out."

"When was this?"

"Few weeks ago." He let out a bitter laugh. "All summer, I'd been picking him up from his place in Palermo and bringing him to Cielo d'Azzurro, *for work*. I didn't know he was in the process of wooing the only girl I'd ever been in love with. All this time, she was telling me no, no, no, but gradually, I'd worn her down. I could feel her opinion of me changing. But then Bruno came in. He pursued her, and she went for it, just like that. Even though he was still married. They were doing it, right under my nose.

"So one day, on our way in from Palermo, he told me. I saw red. Went crazy. I pounded on him. He lost control of the car and we hit the Filardos' old piece of junk. Carmine was pissed. He offered to take care of it, told us to bury whatever grievances we had. I told Bruno it was already forgotten." He shook his head. "But I don't forgive or forget that easy. That's not our family way. When a Piccolo has been wronged, they get even."

"You planned it."

He nodded. "I knew that Capaldi would be there. I knew that Uncle Carmine's been wanting that war with the Capaldi family forever. So I figured I could get rid of Bruno and give the war the push it needed. Two birds, one stone." He shrugged and pointed with his gun. "I just didn't figure on Rafael bringing a meddling little doctor as his guest."

She stiffened. "All right, all right. You killed once. You don't have to do it again. It'll only make things worse for you."

He laughed. "We have plenty of our victims buried on Cielo d'Azzurro. No one knows what happened to them. We'll just add you to the count. Another missing person."

Her stomach dropped as she looked around her. Were the grounds of this gorgeous estate really a cemetery?

"You wouldn't—" But that was silly. Of course he would. He'd done it before. *To his best friend.* She swallowed and tried to sidestep her way behind the statue in the fountain that stood between them. But he stiffened and aimed, so she froze. "That's not going to work. People know I'm here. People who care about me. They'll be asking questions."

He shrugged. "So? Let them. They'll be swept under the rug. It's the same reason no one in town talked when the shooting happened. When the Piccolos act, people know better than to talk about it. They stick their noses where they don't belong, they get them cut off." He smiled. "Like you. You're about to get that pretty little nose of yours cut off, Dottore. And this time, there won't be anybody to help you."

He cocked the gun, aiming it right between her eyes.

She closed her eyes and winced, anticipating the final gunshot, the pain that would end her life.

But instead, the next sensation she experienced was far from either of those things. She felt something furry brush against her calf.

She cracked an eye open and looked down to see Pickle standing beside her, looking up, panting, begging for a treat.

He let out a sharp *yip yip yip* so loud, it pierced the quiet night.

Luigi scowled and dropped the gun's aim to the dog. "Shut up, you stupid rat—"

Suddenly, another voice called out. "Pickle Poo! Where are you, baby?"

There was a far-off commotion, footsteps coming closer, and then someone else, a male voice that seemed to come from right on the other side of the hedge it seemed, said, "Sorry, Patty, he just ran out when I opened the door."

"Oh, he's probably around here somewhere!" she called back, and Pickle yipped again. "Where are you, my little munchkin?"

The words of his beloved seemed to stir Luigi.

He faltered at the sound of her voice, trembling slightly and dropping his aim as he searched the darkness for her.

It gave Audrey the split second she needed to leap forward, dive under the barrel of the gun, and grab his arm.

"What the—" he started as she threw her arms around him and dug her fingers into his injured shoulder. His startled words gave way to a wail of anguish. "Get off of me! *Stupido!*"

He stumbled to the ground, and she fell on top of him, scrabbling for the gun. He still had it in his hand, and he raised it up, trying to aim it at her. She straddled him and grabbed his wrist, trying to wrench it free, but he was too strong for her. With a mighty roar, he threw her off his body, and she went flying back, weightless until her back and shoulders hit the base of the fountain. The impact knocked the wind out of her and sent pain crashing up her spine.

Her vision blurred as she tried to gather the strength to get up. But the pain was too much. Her heels slid along the stone path as she tried to find purchase, something to hold onto so she could push herself to standing. Every nerve in her body protested. It felt like there was nothing but jelly beneath her chin.

Through the haze, she saw Luigi scramble to his feet, gun raised. He aimed it at her and wiped the sweat from his brow. *"Buona notte,"* he murmured, sneering.

Again, she closed her eyes, expecting the gunshot.

When it went off, she winced, knowing there'd be pain, but hoping it'd take her life quickly. But instead, all she felt was a little bit of pressure at her hip, and she heard a hollow clunk.

Then she heard someone scream, "Luigi!" Another clunk, a moan, and then a thud. She opened her eyes in time to see Luigi, slack-jawed and hazy-eyed, collapsing to his knees before pitching over to the ground like a fallen tree.

Behind him, holding a large stone in her hands, part of the edging of the garden, was Patty.

"Oh, my *gawd, Awd,*" she said, wide-eyed, as she dropped the dirty stone and stared in disgust at her dirty hands. "You're lucky I came here when I did. What on Earth was that all about?"

The pressure at her hip gave way to slight numbness. She dropped her hand to her side and felt around for the blood. "I've been shot," she whispered.

CHAPTER TWENTY SIX

Stepping over Luigi's broken body, Patty tottered over to the fountain and sank to her knees beside Audrey. "Where?"

"Here." Audrey lifted the fabric of her cardigan. There was a hole in the bottom of it that hadn't been there before. She put her finger through it, feeling for her hip, but instead felt something hard.

She took it out and looked at it. It was the Piccolo coin, and it'd been merely dented by the bullet, which fell out into her hand as she turned open the pocket. The bullet was more misshapen than the coin. "The Piccolo coin," she whispered. "It saved my life."

Patty gaped at it, then helped Audrey up so that she could sit on its edge. "Are you okay?"

Audrey nodded, rubbing the back of her head. She had a big goose egg there from the impact, but it didn't feel like it was bleeding. The rest of her body was fine, too. No wounds, scrapes, or bruises to speak of.

"I think so . . . *he* killed Bruno. I confronted him on it, and . . . he admitted it, and . . . then he pulled a gun." Her words came out, breathless. "He would've killed me if you hadn't shown up."

She gaped. "No! Not Luigi! It can't be!"

Audrey nodded. "It's true."

"*Gawd*, he did?" She shuddered. "I always thought he wasn't the sharpest fork in the drawer. My poor Bruno. And they were such good friends. Why?"

"Well," she said with a shrug. "You."

Her mouth opened. "Me?"

"He said he's been in love with you for decades. You didn't know?"

"No! Of course not. Oh my *gawd*!" She stood up and marched over to his body. "Luigi! What an idiot! How dare he! He said he loved me?"

Audrey nodded.

"Ew! What a creep! How could he even . . ." She kicked his still body. He started to rouse, moaning, and so she crouched down and picked up the gun. Then she grabbed him by the lapels and pulled him over so that his face was visible. She smacked his cheek with the barrel of the gun. "Wake up. Wake up, stupid."

He moaned some more, and his eyelids fluttered.

She leaned into him and said, "What were you doing, idiot? Killing Bruno? Did you think it would make me like you more? I've never even thought of you that way, dummy! For the last time, you. Are. My. Cousin!" She rolled her eyes and fell backwards onto her rear end, then looked at Audrey. "And then you tried to kill my best friend! This family . . . geesh."

"Distant cousin . . ." he murmured. "Very distant. We're not even blood."

She tightened her hand into a fist and drew back for a punch. "Oh, I'll show you blood." Then she stopped and sighed. "Poor Bruno. So I don't understand. What about Franco? He had nothing to do with it? Luigi made the whole thing up about the shots coming over his head, then?"

Audrey nodded. "Franco is the classic case of wrong place, wrong time. They'd been fighting, and Luigi couldn't take it anymore. He saw his chance while they were walking alone on the side of the road and shot him, but Bruno turned and shot back. They were both injured. So Luigi loaded them both back up in the car and drove back to Cielo d'Azzurro."

Patty looked up at the sky and let out a dramatic sigh. "Unbelievable." Luigi was trying to get up, rubbing his sore head, but she stepped on his shoulder with a kitten heel. "Stay there. I'm sure Carmine will want to deal with you."

He pouted up at her with puppy-dog eyes. His love for her had been so obvious. How hadn't she noticed it before? Audrey would've laughed if she weren't still so shell-shocked, shaking from the events of the past few moments.

Just then, Pickle ran into the clearing, being happily chased by Nick. "There you are!" Patty said, setting the gun down on the edge of the fountain and gathering him up into her arms. "You rascal. You ran away from us."

Nick hopped into Audrey's lap and made himself at home. She pulled a few dried flower petals from his tail. Stroking his warm fur calmed her like nothing else could. When she stood, still carrying him in her arms, she realized how cold it was. The night had brought a definite chill to the air. She shivered.

"Let's go inside," Patty said, noticing.

Audrey looked at Luigi, who was lying there, obediently following Patty's directions. "But what about him?"

Without warning, Patty screamed out, "Sandro! Get over here. The fountain."

Moments later, Alessandro, Rafael, and Rocco emerged from the hedges. "What's going on?" Sandro asked. "What happened to Luigi?"

"He killed Bruno," Audrey said.

Rafael's eyes went wide. "No. It isn't true. Why would he—" He looked at Luigi. "Why would you do something like that? You two were like brothers!"

Luigi looked away from him. "He never let me have anything for myself." He waved a hand at Rafael. "You wouldn't understand. I'm glad he's gone."

"No. I don't understand," Rafael said, waving his hands at him. "And Father is going to have a lot to say to you. You killed one of our own, and you know the penalty for that. He won't protect you just because you are one of us. In fact, it is worse. You know he is going to come down very hard on you, because he trusted you."

Luigi glowered. "Yeah, so? I expect it."

Rafael threw his hands up and shook his head in disappointment. "Ah, Luigi! All these years we've looked after you, only to have you betray us like this. You've really done it this time, and there is nothing I can do to protect you anymore. Get up. Sandro." He motioned to his little brother. "Take him to Father so he can tell him exactly what he's done. I'll be there in a moment."

Sandro reached down and grabbed Luigi by the arm. Luigi stood up and nudged him away, then fixed his sling and tie and slowly followed him, ignoring the glares of everyone present. Rocco and Patty followed suit.

Rafael approached Audrey. "You discovered this? How?"

"It just occurred to me, after we spoke, that it would be really hard for Franco Testo to make that shot. That, combined with the bullet Luigi showed me . . . I realized that I'd made a mistake, blaming Franco," she explained. "And then when I confronted Luigi about it, he admitted it. He'd been in love with Patty all this time. Did you know that?"

He shook his head and rubbed the back of his neck. "In love with Patty? No, I didn't . . . well, to tell you the truth, I never really thought about it." He dragged a hand down his face. "This is going to make my father very unhappy."

"I'm sorry," she said. "I didn't want to—"

"No. It is not your fault."

"Yes—but what's going to happen to Luigi now? Is he going to be punished?"

Rafael nodded. "He'll be dealt with."

"I don't know if I want to know what that means." She shuddered.

"Please, don't worry about that." He placed a hand on each of her shoulders. "In fact, once again, we are in your debt."

"No, really, you're not." She lifted the Piccolo coin and held it up so he could see the dent in it. "I think this calls it even. So we're good."

He eyed it with surprise, then shook his head. "You are quite an extraordinary woman, Audrey. I am glad you came with me on this trip."

"You know what? I am, too." She couldn't believe the words even as she said them, but somehow, she felt it. "As crazy as the past couple days have been . . . it's actually been a lot of fun, sharing this time with your family."

He chuckled. "But correct me if I'm wrong? I think you're ready to go home."

She nodded and smiled up at him. "Absolutely. Just say when."

*

It was after ten when Audrey finished packing her weekend bag and loaded Nick into his carrier. She walked down the staircase to the foyer, the place once again crypt-quiet.

On the second step of the stairs, she looked over at the door to Carmine's office. It was closed, as it had been for the past twenty minutes, when Rafael went inside to confer with Carmine and the rest of the men about Luigi's fate. She could hear faint voices coming from within, but nothing more. Certainly no more gunshots—she'd heard precisely one of those, and never wanted to hear it again.

He'll be dealt with. What did that mean? Luigi had committed the worst crime against the family possible. In the movies, the mafia had a grisly way of bringing people to an end for the mere sin of looking at the don in the wrong way. What kind of punishment would he receive? Was he receiving it now?

Rafael had told her not to worry about it, but she couldn't help it.

She set her bag down at the front door and the pet carrier beside it. Audrey held her breath as she took a step toward the door. She wasn't

151

planning on listening—at least, not since she'd gotten in trouble that last time, but she didn't have the choice. The moment she approached the door, it swung open, and Rafael appeared.

"Audrey," he said. He looked tired. "Are you ready to go?"

She nodded and looked over his shoulder, to see if she could find Luigi. She didn't have to look for long. A moment later, he came out, his head down. He looked as if Carmine had given him a swift tongue-lashing, but physically, he was fine.

He stepped past her without another word and climbed the stairs. She watched him go. "So what will happen to him?"

"Tomorrow, I will take him to the police and explain everything so that Franco Testo can be released. We'll hand him to the justice system to dole out the proper punishment."

"Oh!" And here, she'd been envisioning all sorts of cruel, medieval punishments. "I thought . . ."

"The family can't punish one of its own. He'll be excommunicated from the family, which to most of us is a fate worse than death," he said, shaking his head. "Now, if you'll excuse me, I'll get my bag and meet you outside."

She nodded and watched as he climbed the steps. She was just about to head for the door when a low voice called, "Dottore. Come in."

She turned and saw Carmine behind his desk, beckoning to her.

Audrey stepped inside, holding her breath, wondering just what he would say to her. Maybe he'd be angry at her for preventing the war. Or for outing one of their own as the killer. His face was stone as she approached, leaking no emotion whatsoever.

"Yes?" she asked when she was a few paces from his desk.

He stood up, reached across, and offered his hand. She stared at it. Was she supposed to shake his hand or kiss his ring?

Before she could decide on an answer, he lunged forward, grabbed her hand, and shook it fiercely. "I thank you for everything you have done. As a token of my appreciation, I would like to help you find your father. Rafi says you have been looking for him for quite some time, and—"

"Actually, I appreciate your wanting to help, and I may call upon your help in the future. But right now, I think I have so much going on with my vet practice and renovating my house. I think I should concentrate on that."

He raised an eyebrow. "Are you sure?"

She smiled. "Yes. But it was so very nice to meet you and to be welcomed into your home. You have a lovely family. I thank you for your hospitality."

He came around his desk and unexpectedly pulled her into a great big bear hug. "All right. You know where I am. You take care of my Rafi, would you?"

She nodded, looking into his eyes. He might have been a cold, heartless don, but there was love for his son there, too. "I'll keep an eye on him in Mussomeli, for sure."

When she went out the door, Patty and Sandro were there. He was leaning into her, trying to whisper into her ear. She swatted him away. "For the last time. I'm your cousin, you sick little twerp!" she shouted, splaying a palm on his face and shoving him away.

He shrugged and turned his gaze on Audrey, that wolfish look returning as he ran his eyes up and down her body. "And you, my little American love . . ."

"I'm leaving," she said, extending a hand to him. "Bye."

He took it and kissed her knuckles gently. "Until we meet again?"

"Right." She rolled her eyes.

The moment Sandro let go of her hand, Patty bounced into her arms, giving her a big hug. "I am going to miss you so so so much, Cagney!" She winked. "If you ever need a partner in crime, look me up."

Audrey laughed. "I will. Take care."

She went outside to wait for Rafael, pulling out her phone. She had a text from Concetta that said, *Everything's fine. See you tomorrow?*

She quickly typed in: *Yep. See you then!*

Then she noticed another message, from Mason. It was from an hour ago. It said: *Stopped in to see if you'd made it back. Guess you're not in yet. Doesn't matter how late—give me a call when you get in.*

She smiled at that, and felt something tugging at her. She missed Mussomeli. Missed the vet center, her house, the animals, the town, G's ciambotta, her friends . . . but most of all, she missed Mason. She wanted to see his handsome, smiling face.

But that was rude, considering here she was with Rafael. It wasn't right to play him. But what had Rafael been doing to her? He'd brought her for this weekend trip, and she'd expected that by the end of it, she'd know what his intentions were. But even now, she had no clue.

He came out, threw his bag in the convertible, and raised the top. She sat in the front passenger seat and took one last look at the Piccolo mansion, all lit up. Then they turned for home, heading into complete darkness.

It was a good thing he'd put the top up, because the night was getting chillier and chillier, and there was fog in the air. But Rafael must have driven the route all his life, because he was just as relaxed as ever.

"You think Luigi will be okay?" she asked him as they drove up into the hills.

He nodded. "I think he will be."

"He'll really be cut off from everyone? You'll never talk to him again?"

He shrugged. "That is the way it's supposed to work."

"That must be hard. And it must be hard to be a don, to have to make those decisions based on tradition."

He glanced over at her. "It is hard. I do many things that don't make sense to me, because of my family's tradition. But I get much in return, so I can't complain."

They drove on in silence, and meanwhile, Audrey tried to think of some way to bring up the subject of why he'd agreed to bring her on this trip. By the time they reached the city limits of Mussomeli, she was nearly mad with curiosity.

She blurted, "Do you like me?"

Then she cringed. *Great going, Audrey. Could you sound any more like a twelve-year-old?*

He looked over at her and smiled. "Of course you know the answer to that."

"No." She pouted, wondering how anyone could be so thick. "What I mean is, are you interested in me romantically? Or are you just being friendly?"

"Ah," he said, his hands tightening on the steering wheel. Then, to her surprise, he started to chuckle. "I have confused you, haven't I?"

She nodded, a little hurt by the way he was laughing. Was it funny to see the two of them as a couple? "Your little brother said you probably weren't, but—"

"Sandro is bright. He probably knew before I did," he said, reaching over and putting a hand on hers. "The truth is, I'm not interested in women romantically. I'm gay."

She blinked. "You . . .are?"

He nodded. "My father doesn't know. No one else does either. He wants me to continue this strong Piccolo family, but the thing is, he'd

154

be crushed to know that that is something I am not interested in doing. So maybe I was overdoing it a little bit in front of him, and for that, I am sorry. But I really do value you, and our friendship, so I hope you do not hate me too much?"

She stared at the road ahead, expecting to feel hurt. But instead, she felt nothing but relief. In fact, had she known that he wasn't interested in her that way, she might've had even more fun. "No, it's really okay!" she said with a laugh, squeezing his hand. "Your secret is absolutely safe with me."

"Good. Then we are still friends?" he asked.

She nodded. "Of course we are."

CHAPTER TWENTY SEVEN

Audrey smiled when the stone wall surrounding Rafael's orange grove came into view. It meant that they were almost home. She took a deep breath, letting the cool air into her lungs. It was tinged lightly with citrus, and felt heavenly against her skin.

"You must be tired. Pull into your place. I'll just walk the rest of the way," she said.

"Nonsense. All those steps up to the town? With your luggage and your fox? And don't forget your mirror."

"No, really!" she said. "Please. The weather's so beautiful. I'd really like the walk. And I can manage it all."

He shrugged and pulled down the drive to his villa in the middle of the orange groves. When he stopped the car, she got out and gathered her things. Rafael helped her, then gave her a big hug. "You come back and see me anytime you want, okay?"

"Of course! You're my neighbor, aren't you? And maybe you'll come up to the vet and adopt a pet for this place. You certainly have enough property." Her eyes lit up. "Actually, I think I have the one for you. A dog. He's the sweetest. You'll love him."

He shook her hand. "Sounds like a deal."

She let Nick out of the pet carrier and collapsed it into her luggage, then took the weekend bag in one arm and the mirror in the other. The moonlight was just enough to help light her way up the long staircase to the city proper. Nick scampered along ahead of her, guiding the way.

"Well, Bub, it's good to be home," she told him as she reached the very top step of the staircase. A little winded, she looked around and smiled. Everything was just as she'd left it, but that was the good thing about this town. It'd been largely the same for hundreds of years.

Even though it was late, there was a festival in the main piazza, and people were out in force, talking and enjoying the music and dance. Most smiled at her and said *Buena notte* as she walked past. The windows of all the homes were brightly lit and cozy, and the air smelled of garlic and citrus and freshly made pasta sauce.

As she passed the old ma-and-pa hardware store where she'd acquired most of the goods to fix up her home, the owner, a lady who never smiled, waved her down.

Audrey stopped as the woman gestured wildly with her hands. She said, "Dr. Smart. You have a balance due. Luca came to collect it from you yesterday but you were not at home. You must pay tomorrow or we will charge you a late fee!"

"Oh! I am so sorry, *signora*. I was out of town for the weekend. I will come by first thing tomorrow morning on the way to the clinic and settle my account," she said.

For the first time ever, the woman nodded at her . . . and smiled.

Audrey wished her a good night and headed on, wondering what she'd done to earn that smile. It wasn't until she turned onto her own street and *Piazza Tre* came into view that it hit her.

The owner of the hardware store didn't speak English.

Audrey had spoken that entire thing, without even thinking about it, in Sicilian.

She froze at the thought. All these months, she'd been struggling, listening to lessons online, thinking she'd never get fluent in the language. And now, five months in . . . she was there. Well, not exactly fluent, but making progress.

Giddy, she practically skipped her way to her front door. As she reached it, she noticed that across the street, Nessa's flowerbeds were nothing but dirt. Nessa was sitting on the front stoop, on the phone with someone, shouting for all to hear. "I don't care! Get a gardener in here now!" A pause. "No, *you* listen to me!! I have a blister the size of Texas on my thumb, and it's all because of that stupid garden you're insisting I have. I am done digging in the dirt. That's *gross*! For the last time, I told you from the beginning that I don't have a green thumb, so if you want the house to have flowers, you can put them in yourself. You got me?"

She jabbed at the phone and let out annoyed groan, then kicked open the door and went inside.

Audrey smiled. Just Nessa, up to her old drama. It wouldn't be Mussomeli without it.

When she turned the key in her lock and went inside, she took in her home, seeing it in a new way. Just a few months ago, it had been a squalid hole-in-the-wall. But it had had potential. Now, she was seeing that potential come through. The home wasn't done, but it was getting

157

there. Now, instead of looking over every room, seeing what needed to be done, a sense of relief washed over her. It was good to be back.

She rushed up the stairs and threw her bag on her bed. Then she carefully unwrapped the mirror and held it in place over the broken one in the upstairs bathroom. She grinned. "Perfect!"

She caught sight of Nick, sitting atop the toilet lid, in the reflection of the mirror. "What do you think, Bub?" When he scampered away, she nodded. "Yep. My thoughts exactly. It's a keeper."

She took it down. She'd need to clean it, then go to the store tomorrow morning to get the hardware to hang it, plus she still had to paint the walls. She was thinking a seafoam green, now, instead of the old parchment, to match the little stones in the frame of the mirror. Another couple of days, and it'd be done. She couldn't wait. Then, her bedroom, and then . . . well, who knew what else?

Right now, she had enough on her hands.

As she went to her bedroom to change, someone rapped on the door. It was a quick, familiar knock, and she knew exactly who it was. Mason.

Suddenly, she remembered his text, and that she was supposed to have called him when she got in. She rushed down the stairs and opened the door, breathless, for more than one reason.

He just made her that way. Every time she looked at him, he seemed to grow more handsome. "Hi," she said.

He looked a little hurt. "Did you just get in?"

She nodded. "Yeah. I was about to text you. I was a little worried it was too late, though. I didn't want to—"

"No, no." He smiled crookedly. "I wanted to let you know the plumber should be out tomorrow, so don't use this bathroom in the meantime. How was the trip?"

"Thank you so much for doing that. You saved my life . . . again. It was an adventure, to say the least." She poked her head out. "No Polpetto?"

"Nah." He dug his hands in the pockets of his jeans and pitched back and forth from heel to toe. It looked like there was something on his mind, but he didn't speak.

"Are you okay?" she finally asked.

He nodded, but again, stayed mute.

The cold air was getting in, and he was wearing nothing more than a T-shirt, so she reached out and dragged him inside. "Oh. Come on up. I want you to see what I got on the trip." She ran up the stairs with him at her heels. "There was this antiques shop. Well, more like a junk shop, and I got a new mirror for the bathroom. What do you think of this?"

When she held it up to him, he nodded. "Pretty cool." He looked around. "You do the tile here?"

"Yep. Thanks for cleaning up after the overflow. It doesn't look so bad."

"No, hey. I thought you got a professional to do the tiling. You sure learned a thing or two since the downstairs bathroom."

She laughed. "Thanks to you."

"You're a good learner."

He smiled down at her, and once again, she found them staring, speechless at one another, as if there was so much they had to say, but neither was quite ready to take the plunge. She pointed to the wall. "At first, I was thinking old parchment. Kind of a yellowish? But now I'm thinking of seafoam green. For the walls? I have a valance for the window that's rose-colored, but I think it might work anyhow."

"Yeah. That'll look great."

Once again, a long pause of awkwardness. She pointed down the narrow staircase. "You want to have a glass of wine?"

"No. Nah. I just wanted to make sure you were all set with the plumber and everything. So . . . the trip was good?"

She nodded. She'd said that before. But as she studied him, she realized he was searching for something, and remembered the way he'd looked when Rafael had shown up the other day. He'd been so upset, the tips of his ears had gone red.

Oh. Now she understood. "It's not what you're thinking. Rafael is just a friend. We're not together. If that's what you were wondering about?"

He put up his hands, claiming innocence. "No, I never said—"

"I mean, originally, that was what scared me, aside from the whole mafia thing. But that's not what I want. I don't—I really don't feel that way about him. Or actually, any Sicilian so far."

His eyes flashed to hers. "Any Sicilian?"

She nodded. "That's right."

He hitched both shoulders and gave her a shy look. "What about an American?"

She shrugged and grinned at him. "Oh, I don't know. It's possible."

He chuckled. She'd hoped that might open a window to him, but instead, he turned around and headed down the narrow staircase. But when he reached the door, he turned on her suddenly.

"Look," he said. "I know we've been dancing around this issue for months. But I didn't lie to you when I told you I have a thing for you. More than a thing. I don't want to ruin what we got, but I think you like me, too. So maybe we should give it a try. See where things go? Because—"

"Yes."

He stopped abruptly. "You said yes?"

She nodded, then stood on her tiptoes and planted a kiss right on his mouth.

When she pulled away, he looked at her, dazed and delighted. "Where did that come from?" he said, breathless.

She shrugged. "I got tired of waiting for you to do it."

"You were waiting?"

"Yeah. Hello? *Forever.*"

He smiled. "Well, that didn't work. 'Cause I all but missed it. Don't you know, where I come from in the South, we like to do things slow?" He slipped an arm around her waist and pulled her toward him. "Come here."

And then he pulled her close, swept his lips across hers, sweet and sultry, until she could barely feel the rest of her body. This time, when he pulled away, it was she who was dazed. "Dinner tomorrow?" she asked.

He pumped a fist like a teenager. "Heck yes." He opened the door, stepped outside, and turned around. "See you, Boston."

She waved, still feeling tingles from head to toe. "Not if I see you first."

Closing the door, she jogged upstairs to unpack. The worst part of any trip—laundry. As she pulled her dirty things out of her bag, her phone buzzed with a text from Sabrina. *You asleep?*

She did the math in her head. It was nearly midnight in Sicily, which meant it was six in the evening in Boston. Still excited from everything that had happened and eager to put off the laundry, she jumped into bed and dialed her sister's number. "Nope," she said when she answered.

"Oh, thank goodness. You home?" Sabrina asked with a long yawn. "I have to talk to someone. You will not believe the day I've had!"

"Tell me all about it," Audrey said, settling into her bed and pulling the covers around her. As she did, she looked around and smiled.

Yes. She was home.

NOW AVAILABLE!

BEACHFRONT BAKERY: A KILLER CUPCAKE
(A Beachfront Bakery Cozy Mystery—Book 1)

"Very entertaining. I highly recommend this book to the permanent library of any reader that appreciates a very well written mystery, with some twists and an intelligent plot. You will not be disappointed. Excellent way to spend a cold weekend!"
--Books and Movie Reviews, Roberto Mattos (regarding Murder in the Manor)

BEACHFRONT BAKERY: A KILLER CUPCAKE is the debut novel in a charming and hilarious new cozy mystery series by #1 bestselling author Fiona Grace, whose bestselling Murder in the Manor (A Lacey Doyle Cozy Mystery) has nearly 200 five star reviews.

Allison Sweet, 34, a sous chef in Los Angeles, has had it up to here with demeaning customers, her demanding boss, and her failed love life. After a shocking incident, she realizes the time has come to start life fresh and follow her lifelong dream of moving to a small town and opening a bakery of her own.

When Allison spots a charming, vacant storefront on the boardwalk near Venice, she wonders if she could really start life anew. Feeling like it's a sign, and a time to take a chance in life, she goes for it.

Yet Allison did not anticipate the wild ride ahead of her: the boardwalk, filled with fun and outrageous characters, is pulsing with life, from the Italian pizzeria owners on either side of her who vie for her affection, to the fortune tellers and scheming rival bakery owner nearby. Allison yearns to just focus on her delicious new pastry recipes and keep her struggling bakery afloat—but when a murder occurs right near her shop, everything changes.

Implicated, her entire future at stake, Allison has no choice but to investigate to clear her name. As an orphaned dog wanders into her life, a devoted new sidekick with a knack for solving mysteries, she starts her search.

Will they find the killer? And can her struggling bakery survive?

A hilarious cozy mystery series, packed with twists, turns, romance, travel, food and unexpected adventure, the BEACHFRONT BAKERY series will keep you laughing and turning pages late into the night as you fall in love with an endearing new character who will capture your heart.

Books #2 (A MURDEROUS MACAROON), #3 (A PERILOUS CAKE POP), #4 (A DEADLY DANISH), #5 (A TREACHEROUS TART), and book #6 (A CALAMITOUS COOKIE) are also available!

Fiona Grace

Debut author Fiona Grace is author of the LACEY DOYLE COZY MYSTERY series, comprising nine books; of the TUSCAN VINEYARD COZY MYSTERY series, comprising seven books; of the DUBIOUS WITCH COZY MYSTERY series, comprising three; of the BEACHFRONT BAKERY COZY MYSTERY series, comprising six books; and of the CATS AND DOGS COZY MYSTERY series, comprising six books.

Fiona would love to hear from you, so please visit www.fionagraceauthor.com to receive free ebooks, hear the latest news, and stay in touch.

BOOKS BY FIONA GRACE

LACEY DOYLE COZY MYSTERY
MURDER IN THE MANOR (Book#1)
DEATH AND A DOG (Book #2)
CRIME IN THE CAFE (Book #3)
VEXED ON A VISIT (Book #4)
KILLED WITH A KISS (Book #5)
PERISHED BY A PAINTING (Book #6)
SILENCED BY A SPELL (Book #7)
FRAMED BY A FORGERY (Book #8)
CATASTROPHE IN A CLOISTER (Book #9)

TUSCAN VINEYARD COZY MYSTERY
AGED FOR MURDER (Book #1)
AGED FOR DEATH (Book #2)
AGED FOR MAYHEM (Book #3)
AGED FOR SEDUCTION (Book #4)
AGED FOR VENGEANCE (Book #5)
AGED FOR ACRIMONY (Book #6)
AGED FOR MALICE (Book #7)

DUBIOUS WITCH COZY MYSTERY
SKEPTIC IN SALEM: AN EPISODE OF MURDER (Book #1)
SKEPTIC IN SALEM: AN EPISODE OF CRIME (Book #2)
SKEPTIC IN SALEM: AN EPISODE OF DEATH (Book #3)

BEACHFRONT BAKERY COZY MYSTERY
BEACHFRONT BAKERY: A KILLER CUPCAKE (Book #1)
BEACHFRONT BAKERY: A MURDEROUS MACARON (Book #2)
BEACHFRONT BAKERY: A PERILOUS CAKE POP (Book #3)
BEACHFRONT BAKERY: A DEADLY DANISH (Book #4)
BEACHFRONT BAKERY: A TREACHEROUS TART (Book #5)
BEACHFRONT BAKERY: A CALAMITOUS COOKIE (Book #6)

CATS AND DOGS COZY MYSTERY
A VILLA IN SICILY: OLIVE OIL AND MURDER (Book #1)

A VILLA IN SICILY: FIGS AND A CADAVER (Book #2)
A VILLA IN SICILY: VINO AND DEATH (Book #3)
A VILLA IN SICILY: CAPERS AND CALAMITY (Book #4)
A VILLA IN SICILY: ORANGE GROVES AND VENGEANCE (Book #5)
A VILLA IN SICILY: CANNOLI AND A CASUALTY (Book #6)